Cynthia T. Toney

10 Steps to Girlfriend Status

Bird Face • Book Two

10 Steps to Girlfriend Status

© 2015 Cynthia T. Toney

ISBN-13: 978-1-938092-64-0
ISBN-10: 1938092643

e-Book ISBN-13: 978-1-938092-65-7

This book is a work of fiction. Names, characters, places, and incidents are either products of the author's imagination or used fictitiously. Any similarity to actual people and/or events is purely coincidental.

Published by Write Integrity Press, 2631 Holly Springs Parkway, Box 35, Holly Springs, GA 30142.

www.WriteIntegrity.com

Printed in the United States of America.

Dedication

To teens everywhere.

Know how wonderful and powerful God made you.

Acknowledgements

While the first Bird Face story took ten years to write, this second book took only six months. I owe that speedy delivery in part to the knowledge I gained through working with two ACFW critique groups: Scribes 206 (The Clubhouse, led by Burton Cole) and Scribes 220 (The Scriblerians, led by Tim Akers). They provided a lot of fun, too.

If I could present a medal to Tracy Ruckman, publisher of Write Integrity Press, I would. Her hard work and commitment to her authors is amazing, and that is no exaggeration.

Last, but not least, I am grateful to my husband, Patrick Toney, for his mastery on my website in the face of numerous changes and his dedication as my chauffeur to any event or for any errand pertaining to my books.

Chapter 1

Who would've guessed that looking through old photo albums could get me into so much trouble?

It happened to be Friday—the day before the wedding. No, not mine! I'm only fourteen, and this is Louisiana, not New Hampshire.

I arrived on time at LeMoyne High School, via the Mom-mobile, wearing a skirt that made the best of summer's leftover tan. Baseball-player and heart-throbbing hunk David Griffin leaned against a tree on the front lawn.

Steps toward achieving girlfriend status:

1. Meeting before school (Check.)

We'd known each other since last year, but at the start of ninth grade our friendship expanded like a Cajun cornbread hushpuppy in hot oil.

"Hey, Wendy. TGIF," he shouted.

Man, his grin killed me. "TGI-uh-TD-uh-BTW," I countered. It was really hard to concentrate when he was all I could see.

He burst out laughing and ran a hand over his curly brown hair. "What?"

"Thank goodness it's the day before the wedding." Like

always, heat crept into my cheeks as I drew near him. I smiled big to camouflage the reason.

"Yeah, and I'll be there with a tie and everything." His green eyes dazzled me. "Unless you un-invite me."

"Not a chance. I need all the moral support I can get." I'd never tell him Mom allowed me to invite no more than two friends, and he was one of them. If he only knew how much I looked forward to seeing him away from his jock buddies.

We started up the steps to the main entrance as the first leaves of autumn danced across our path in the warm breeze.

"Well, I might mess up somehow and make you mad today." He stuck an arm out and prevented someone who was coming down the steps from running into me.

"You won't wiggle out that easily."

We reached an intersection of halls and turned in opposite directions.

"See you later," he said over his shoulder.

It took every ounce of willpower not to look back at him as he walked away. But too many pairs of eyes watched, belonging to too many of his friends and teammates who'd poke and tease him.

We weren't a couple—at least not yet. Why invite ridicule or ruin my chances? LeMoyne was three times the size of Bellingrath Junior High, and to say there were a lot of pretty girls here was an understatement of gross proportions.

About a third of the girls had familiar faces. The skinny

and fashionable Sticks paraded the halls like they had in eighth grade, though without the same clout they enjoyed at Bellingrath. Tookie Miller, once their fearless leader, overcame her eating disorder and never returned to them. At LeMoyne she found new friends, including me, which I wouldn't have dreamed of a year ago when she went after David. But my two besties were track buddies Alice Rend and Gayle Freeman, and I'd gotten lucky with a locker assignment between theirs.

"Are you nervous about the wedding?" Gayle, in a blue t-shirt and yellow shorts that showed off her dark brown arms and legs, had passed me up in height since eighth grade. She never looked nervous, not even before the high jump at a track meet.

"Only about doing that slow walk up the aisle in heels." That was a lie. I broke out in a sweat just thinking of my whole new life about to begin.

"Don't worry, girl. I'll stand you back up if you go down." Her full lips stretched into a wide smile. She swatted a bouncy black ringlet off her face and opened her locker door. Taped to the inside was last year's class picture of John Wilson—previously known to me as John-Monster—who'd committed suicide in August. Anyone who dared tease or even question Gayle about his photo received a cold-as-ice glare from her normally warm cocoa-brown eyes.

"Hey, Gayle, are you messin' with my new sister?" Alice sauntered toward us, her blue eyes laughing. Color flooded her pale pink cheeks against her strawberry-blonde hair. "Starting tomorrow, anyway." She set her clarinet case on the floor and dug around in her locker, producing some sheet music.

I smiled. I couldn't think of a sweeter girl to have for a sister. She'd surprised me with a book about Vincent van Gogh for my birthday back when she hardly knew me. "I'm so ready for the wedding to be over. My bags are already packed for tomorrow night."

While Mom and Mr. Rend—there, I did it again. I couldn't stop calling him Mr. Rend. "Think of something else to call him," Mom had said. Not Dad, of course. I had one of those, although I loved Mr. Rend too. And calling him Daniel or Dan didn't seem right. Maybe Pop … Anyway, while *they* went on their honeymoon to the Bahamas, I'd spend my time at the Rends' house. Alice and I would babysit her six-year-old brother, Adam, and when the adults returned in a week, we'd all move together to the new house.

Instant big family. Funny how you wish for something forever, and when it's finally about to happen, your stomach ties into a knot.

"Wendy, come sit with us." Jennifer waved me over to the ballerina table at lunch. It wasn't really a table full of ballerinas, only the one where Jen and a few other members of the classical dance club sat at one end.

I held up an index finger to signal Alice and Gayle, sitting at our usual table, that I'd only be a minute. They nodded and waved me an approval to stay. They accepted the fact that Jennifer was still a part of my life.

"I received an invitation to your mom's wedding." Jennifer gathered her long golden hair into a low ponytail before picking up her fork and stabbing a salad.

"Great! Mom said she was mailing you one. Are you coming?" Best friends in elementary school and junior high, Jen and I seldom saw each other outside of school anymore. Our interests had taken different paths over the summer.

"No, I'm sorry." She stuck out her lower lip. "There's a rehearsal with the ballet theatre I can't get out of, but my parents will be there."

"Oh, I'm really gonna miss you," I girly-whined, then returned to my normal voice. "But I understand. Let me know when your performances are, okay? I'll try to make one of those."

A scraping sound alerted me, and a tray slid toward us from the opposite end of the table.

"Hey!" With a quick hand, I stopped it from crashing into my lunch. I scowled—until I saw David.

"Told you I'd see you later."

"That's a pretty generic phrase."

"Not when I use it." He ambled over to his tray and pulled out the chair next to mine.

Jennifer raised her eyebrows and squeezed her lips

together in a stifled grin. The other ballerinas gawked at David. He nodded at Jen but ignored the rest.

Steps toward achieving girlfriend status:

2. Eating lunch together (Check.)

While ignoring pretty girls? (Bonus Check!)

After school, my next-door neighbor Mrs. Villaturo and I squished together on the sagging middle of her antique sofa, the fabric printed with so many flowers it made me dizzy. This was my last chance to visit with her as neighbors before Mom and Mr. Rend/Daniel/Dan/Pop (boy, I was tired of that) got married and we moved a couple of miles away.

The oven buzzer sounded, and Mrs. V darted to the kitchen. She returned in a minute with a plate of her fabulous chocolate chip cookies and placed it on the coffee table. "Here you go, Wendy." She swept a wayward silver-gray hair off her damp forehead with the back of one hand.

The aroma of my favorite cookies practically sent me to heaven. I grabbed a melty cookie and took a bite that demolished half of it. "Mmphh. Thanksh, Mrsh-sh. V." I caught a falling morsel in my hand and popped it into my mouth.

Her laughter tinkled like a tiny bell as she hoisted a bulky navy-blue photo album from the end table. She sat next to me again and placed the album on her tiny lap. "Let me show you the latest photos of Sarah and Sam."

Sarah and Sam, the grandchildren in Alaska. I'd heard their names and looked at their photos for the eight years I'd lived next door, but I'd never met either of them. "Sure, hang on." I wiped my fingers on a paper napkin and took a swig from my water bottle. I didn't go anywhere without water anymore in case I wanted to take off running on a pretty day.

Mrs. V plunked the album's back section open across my knees. "Here's Sarah on the balance beam at her last gymnastics meet. She's ten now."

"Cute." Skinny legs like mine at her age, but with solid calf and thigh muscles developing. I took in Sarah's other shots behind their plastic sleeves.

Mrs. V flipped the page. "And you remember Sam."

I blinked, then stared. My eyeballs must've bugged out. This was wiry, girly-faced, scabby-kneed Sam? The last photo I'd seen of him, in a baggy soccer uniform, was probably … six months ago. Same sandy blond hair, but that's about all. He squinted one eye above high cheekbones and wrinkled his nose at the camera, his white t-shirt-covering wide shoulders, hands stuffed into the pockets of his jeans.

"Are you okay?" Mrs. V leaned forward and turned her face to the side and upward into mine.

"Oh. Yes." I raised a hand and smoothed my hair back from my warming cheek.

"He's handsome, isn't he?" Mrs. V winked.

"Um-hm." I smiled a tiny, polite smile while I recovered.

Sometimes I could be such an idiot. "He sure has changed a lot."

"So have you over the summer. He started ninth grade this year too."

"Really." I hadn't paid much attention to Mrs. V's chatter about Sam in the past.

"Gus thinks that Sam looks like he did at this age." She nodded toward a brown recliner on the other side of the room, its leather cracked, oily stains on the headrest and arms.

A shiver crept up my spine as I eyed the recliner. "You mean ... Mr. Villaturo?" As in your dead husband?

Love radiated from her face, beautiful in that old-person kind of way. "Don't you notice the resemblance? The same chin, the same smile."

I'd never met Gus. I cut my eyes toward the empty chair again. Did she really see him sitting there, or did she only remember something he'd said years ago?

Mrs. V smiled. "Sometimes Gus says, 'Ana, it's time to go visit our little Gus again.'" She looked back at the recliner. "Don't you, Gus?"

And it hit me—she must be so lonely. Could that be what caused her to imagine him? Nobody visited her but me, and I hadn't been able to stop by in the past few weeks. I'd been super busy with school, the wedding, and the upcoming move.

My heart ached for her—the nearest thing to a grandmother I had. We'd spent so much time together, even volunteering as a team for the local animal rescue organization. Other than Mom and Dad, no adult had devoted so much time to me or meant more to me than she did.

I touched her arm. "Maybe we should look at some more photos, Mrs. V."

She pulled her focus from the recliner back to the album.

Using my softest tone, I said, "I have to go soon. There's a lot to do for the wedding, and I promised Mom I'd finish packing up my room."

"Oh, dear, I forgot to offer you some tea." She was herself again, Gus's chair just another piece of furniture. She got up and scurried to the kitchen once more before I could refuse. "With honey, the way you like it," she shouted behind her.

I did a fast calculation, adding the years since her only birthday party I remembered, and figured Mrs. V was at least seventy-five years old. So what did I just witness? A moment of forgetfulness, senility—or something else?

My excitement over the wedding and moving into a big new house drained out of me like someone punched a hole in my bucket.

"Now that didn't take long, did it?" She set two steaming mugs of tea next to the cookie plate.

Her fingers barely let go of the mug handles before I reached up and hugged her.

"Oh!" She wobbled and landed with her rear end on the sofa, grabbing my arms to steady herself.

"I love you, Mrs. V, and I'll miss you so much after I move. But I'll ride my bike over here to see you as often as I can." I let go of her little body, so fragile.

"I love you too, Wendy. I know you'll do your best." She smiled, wrinkles gathering in familiar clusters on her face.

Tears built behind my lids, and something tore at my insides. If only she were my real grandmother and could move with us.

We each took a sip of tea as though to speed past our sadness—at least hers was a sip. Mine was a slurp, a bit too hot, but it stopped the tears. I stood up and stretched while I blinked them away.

She picked up another photo album, black and tattered and much thinner than the first. One I hadn't seen before.

I took a deep breath. "Just a few more, okay?"

She opened the album to pages that were brown and crumbling. "Did your parents ever tell you about the scandal?"

The thrill of learning a secret rushed through me. "Scandal?" I sat down again.

"Your grand-mere Robichaud and I knew each other when we were girls. She was a Broussard, as you probably know."

I nodded.

"I had cousins in her town, Bayou Calmon, and I visited them almost every summer."

"You did?" Strange that she waited so long to tell me she knew Grand-mere.

"Here's a picture of Odette and me." She tapped a fingertip on a blurry, faded photo held to the page by black paper triangles on the corners.

"How cute." They stood side by side, arms entwined, Grand-mere the taller of the two.

"She called me Peeshwank, Cajun for *runt*. How I hated that." Mrs. V laughed and shook her head.

Apparently I wouldn't be able to hurry her to the juicy stuff, so I settled further into the sofa. "Who's that boy in the background?" His skin was a deeper color than that of the girls, as though he spent a lot of time outdoors.

"That's Odette's older brother, your great-uncle Andre."

Andre. "That was the name of my great-grandfather. You're saying he had a son by that name?"

She perked up like she was about to answer but instead grinned and waved at someone outside a window. "Look, Gus is working in the yard. He so loves to keep busy."

From where we sat, I scanned through the windows and sliding glass door, their curtains pulled back. Chanceaux, the dog Jen and I cared for and Mrs. V adopted after it was abandoned in our neighborhood, napped on the patio. But no one was working in the yard. Not today, anyway. And especially not Gus Villaturo.

Something more than loneliness was doing this to her, and it wasn't just creeping me out anymore. Maybe this was the symptom of a serious problem I needed to tell someone about.

But should I leave her alone? "Mrs. V, do you feel okay?"

"As fine as ever." Her voice held a cheerful lilt.

I smiled and squeezed her hand. "Then I'll see you at the wedding tomorrow, right?" I prayed she could still drive herself safely.

"Of course! I have a new dress and hat to show off."

The scandal story would have to wait, if there really was a scandal. The way Mrs. V acted, maybe she was sick and confused. I picked up my water bottle, headed to the door, and then turned and wiggled my fingers in good-bye. Only I wasn't exactly sure anymore who the person was that waved back.

Still puzzled over Mrs. V's behavior, I walked from her house, through my gate, and to the kitchen door in under a minute. Belle, my yellow Labrador mix—one of Chanceaux's puppies found with her last spring—followed me in.

Mom and Mr. Rend huddled at the table. Her dark head and his blond one bent over an assortment of wedding notes, travel brochures, and house details for the millionth time.

Not a good idea to interrupt.

"Wendy, dinner's going to be late." Mom's messy hair gave me a clue as to her emotional state: frazzled. "But Belle's already eaten."

"Okay, Mom. I can make a sandwich."

Mr. Rend raised his eyes and smiled, his face turning bright pink. So like his daughter, Alice. I smiled back but didn't address him as anything. We were in that awkward day-before-the-wedding state where whatever I called him would probably change after we settled into a house together. I'd figure out something to call him soon enough.

I slapped some deli turkey between two slices of bread, wrapped the sandwich in a paper towel, and made a beeline for my room. Belle trailed after me.

In thirty-eight hours, if all went according to plan, my last name would no longer be the same as my mother's. Or the same as anyone else's in our new household. I'd be the oddball, one Robichaud thrown in with four Rends.

For the eight years since Dad left, it had been only Mom and me. I'd often wished for a whole family again, so why did I feel so unsure now that I was actually going to have one? I sighed and placed the sandwich on my dresser.

My pink bridesmaid dress hung on a hook outside my closet. I stripped down and slipped it over my head like I'd done every day since I got it last week. I ran jittery palms over my tummy and hips, smoothing the formfitting satin skirt.

David had said he liked me in pink when I wore a pink t-shirt to school. It was the perfect color for my dark brown hair and ivory skin, he insisted. I swallowed to calm the butterflies that rose in my chest. After he said that, I didn't care if I ever got another tan. But running outdoor track this spring in a tank and shorts, I would.

Alice's dress was the same style as mine but in pastel

blue. Great for her strawberry blonde hair and pale pink skin, which she protected with sunscreen when she ran. More pink would've been a disaster on her.

The front door of the house closed and its deadbolt clicked, followed by a car engine coming to life. Mr. Rend was heading back to his place. Good thing. I needed some quiet time with Mom.

Wearing the bridesmaid dress, I peeked into her room. She stood in front of a full-length mirror in the suit she'd chosen to be married in. The fabric was cream color with pinstripes of pink and blue crisscrossing each other. Windowpane plaid, she called it. Retro styling, of course, like her taste in everything from kitchen utensils to furniture. A straight knee-length skirt and a three-quarter-sleeve jacket, double-breasted, with an open neckline and shawl collar. Very 1960s. Very First Lady Jackie Kennedy.

She turned toward me and burst out laughing. "You couldn't resist either, could you?" She waved me in. "Come over here, you gorgeous thing."

I breezed into the room and stood beside her in front of the mirror. "You look great, Mom." We squeezed hands.

"Only one more night for our little family of two." Her eyes moistened at the description she'd used for us since the divorce.

I sighed and nodded.

"Is there anything you want to talk about while we still

have some time alone?" She looked me in the eye as she removed her matching cream-colored heels.

Reluctant, I gritted my teeth but then spilled it, my voice low. "Actually, there is. It's about Mrs. V."

"Oh? This sounds rather serious."

"Yeah, I think it is."

"Want to sit?"

"I don't want to wrinkle." I reached for my zipper, and Mom helped me out of my dress. She draped it over her chair, and I plopped on the bench at the end of the bed.

She unbuttoned her jacket and hung it on a padded hanger.

I took a deep breath. "I hate to bring this up right before your big day, but I'm worried."

"It's okay. Tell me what's going on."

"When I was at Mrs. V's this afternoon, she acted like she saw her dead husband, Gus." I swallowed. "Twice."

Mom crinkled her eyes and pressed her lips together like it hurt to hear that. "She's getting pretty old, honey."

"I know. My guess is about seventy-five." I lowered my gaze to my hands resting in my lap. "I'm looking forward to living with the Rends, but it's so sad for Mrs. V to be by herself. And I'm scared for her."

"I understand. This concerns me too." She rubbed my shoulder. "We'll continue to watch out for her the best we can."

I placed my hand on hers. "Okay." But I wasn't

convinced. Although she'd quit her job, Mom would be super busy after the wedding taking care of three more people. "I told her I'd still visit her."

"Of course. And I'll let her son in Alaska know about this. She gave me his phone number in case of emergency."

True, she had a son. Surely, he cared about her, so maybe I was letting this worry me too much. "Thanks, Mom." I kissed her cheek. "Well, I'm still working on my room, so ..."

She reached behind her, unzipped and wiggled out of her skirt. "Let me know if anything else is bothering you. Even after I'm married." She grinned, standing in her slip.

"I will." I grabbed my dress and started for the door but then turned to face her again. "Mom, did Grand-mere Robichaud have a brother?"

The color drained from her face. "Why do you ask?" She had the same expression as when I was five years old, still sucking my thumb, and wanted to know what happened to my ratty old baby blankie.

"Mrs. V showed me an old photo of her and Grand-mere in Bayou Calmon. There was a boy in the background, and Mrs. V said he was Grand-mere's older brother, Andre."

Mom focused on clipping her skirt to its hanger before answering. "I heard she had a brother I never met. You would have to ask your dad about him, but don't be surprised if he doesn't want to talk."

I had two options: try to pull information out of Dad or

question Mrs. V when I visited her again. Based on Mom's reaction, Dad might not be a wise choice. I'd take my chances with Mrs. V.

Close to bedtime, Belle followed my movements with her big brown eyes as I boxed some things to be picked up by the moving van the week after next.

"Don't worry, girl. We'll take your bed and bowls to the Rends' house tomorrow morning, and I'll meet you there after the wedding." I kissed the top of her honey-colored head as she thumped her tail against the floor.

I plucked all the art off my bedroom walls and stacked it in boxes. From the bulletin board above my desk, I removed the snapshots taken during eighth grade, some of Jennifer and me. A few were from the Spring Program, including shots of my scenery art for our production of *Oklahoma*.

That weekend had been the loneliest and most miserable of my life, when I let my envy of Jennifer cause me to treat her so horribly. I never wanted to feel that lonely again. But would I miss being able to *be alone*? As much as I loved Alice and Adam already, I didn't know if I wanted them around every minute of every day. And I was used to answering only to Mom. What would having a stepfather be like?

Mom rapped at my door. "Wendy?"

I swung it open wide. "Hey. What's up?"

"I wanted to let you know that I phoned Mrs. V's son, and

he's coming down to see her next week. His name is Tony, in case you run into him before I do."

My spirits lifted a little. "Thanks for taking the time to do that, Mom, in spite of the wedding and all."

"Well, I know how you are, and I didn't want you to worry the whole week I was gone." She smiled and stepped back to leave.

"Love you, Mom." I smiled back and started to push the door closed again.

She stopped it with the flat of her hand. "Oh, and he's bringing his son, Sam."

Chapter 2

If I had to be the first one to say it, Alice and I looked great at the wedding.

She wore her hair up in a figure-eight swirl that I helped her create. Peach lip gloss and pale blue eye shadow worked with her blue dress.

For my hair, a gold barrette pulled the sides away from my face but left it hanging down the back. Orchid-colored eye shadow brought out the green flecks in my brown eyes. For lipstick, I went with a deeper shade of the pink in my dress.

David parked himself up front in the second pew of the church. Each time I glanced his way from my position next to the altar, he was staring a hole through me. He wore a pale pink shirt with his suit. That couldn't have been an accident.

Standing next to me, Alice fingered her mother's aquamarine birthstone pendant at her throat. She caught me staring and shot me a sideways look. That sadness in her eyes only showed up when she missed her mother, who'd died before Mr. Rend left the Air Force and moved Alice and Adam to Louisiana. It had to be hard to see her dad fall in love with someone else. I'd been in that spot. And she must've been just as afraid as I was about the unknown—having a new parent. I closed my hand around her fist that held her bouquet of white roses and smiled.

She nodded. We were in this together.

When the priest gave his final blessing, the newly married couple kissed. Mom's face beamed like I'd never seen before, not even after a successful salvage hunt at the local flea market. Not even the day she found a marble-top end table on the side of the road.

I lifted the gold crucifix inherited from Grand-mere Robichaud from around my neck and kissed it.

David's eyes met mine, and I smiled at him until I moved down the aisle and he disappeared from view. Gayle leaned from her pew so I'd spot her grinning like her face would split, and I grinned back and waved my bouquet in the air. Mrs. V stood a few feet behind Gayle wearing so blank an expression I couldn't begin to imagine what she was thinking. As soon as possible at the reception, I needed to find Mrs. V again.

Our limousines drove the wedding party two blocks to the reception hall, and some of the guests traveled the short distance on foot. Without a driver's license between them, David and Gayle must've been among the walkers. That gave me a moment to dab sweat off my upper lip with a tissue and take a deep breath in the receiving line before—

"Hey, you look great." David appeared out of nowhere.

I gasped. "Hey!" I said a little too loudly and then giggled.

With his suit coat draped over one arm, he reached for my hand and kissed me on the cheek.

A warm, tingling wave spread outward from the spot where his lips touched my skin. It left me speechless.

Steps toward achieving girlfriend status:

3. Hand holding (Check.)

4. Cheek kissing (Check.)

"I'll see you when you're done." David moved on to Alice and then to the bride and groom.

Mrs. Nguyen stepped up to me and began chattering in heavily accented English about how beautiful the flowers looked.

By the time Alice and I finished greeting everyone who came through the line, we groaned and kicked off our heels. I dropped mine next to the nearest empty chair and collapsed into it. Alice took off to stop Adam from running his finger through the icing on the groom's cake for the second time.

She must get tired of looking out for him.

"Thirsty?" David stood before me with a cup of punch in his hand.

"Yes." I accepted and took a big swallow. "Thanks so much."

"So how do you like my shirt?" He pinched and pulled it away from his chest as though I couldn't see it otherwise.

"I like it. Wherever did you get the idea for a color like that?" I widened my eyes.

He grinned and sat down next to me.

I sighed, stretched my legs out front, and flexed my ankles.

"Don't get too comfortable."

"Why not?"

"We have to dance when the music starts."

"We do?"

As though on cue, the bandleader spoke into his microphone. "Congratulations to Mr. and Mrs. Daniel Rend. Let's give them a big round of applause as they begin their first dance as husband and wife."

I set my cup on the floor and clapped along with the crowd. The music started, a Big Band number, and I turned to David. "What would you call your stepfather?"

His eyebrows practically twisted into a knot, and I laughed. "I mean, if you suddenly gained a stepfather, but you still had a father you saw regularly like I do, what would you call him?"

"His name's Daniel, right?"

I nodded.

"What's he like?"

"Well, he used to be in the military."

"Then I'd call him 'sir.'"

I punched his arm. "I'm serious."

"So am I." He rubbed his arm but laughed. "Does he have a good sense of humor?"

Mr. Rend and Alice's personalities were similar. Sort of
... mellow. "He doesn't tell jokes, if that's what you mean. But
he laughs at funny stuff."

"Big Dan. Dan Man. Dan-O. Ever watch Hawaii Five-O?"
I shook my head.

"Papa Dan."

"That sounds like he makes pizza."

David raised his hands. "My brainstorming is over."

"Maybe 'Papa D.'" Sounded affectionate enough. He'd
probably like it. "Thanks, David. You actually helped."

"You're surprised? That's why I'm here." He stood and
extended his hand toward me. "Time for our dance."

Mom and Papa D had finished dancing, and a new slow
number began—Moonlight Serenade by Glenn Miller. Gayle
and Alice paired with some guests of the Rends and moved to
the middle of the floor. I glanced down at my high heels lying
on their sides and then into David's face.

"Shoes optional." He wiggled his fingers, beckoning me.

I placed my hand in his and walked onto the dance floor in
bare feet. My eyes were level with his mouth. I wrapped my
left arm around his shoulder.

He took small steps and avoided crushing my toes. I
leaned into him and closed my eyes, letting my forehead touch
his jaw. The music washed over me, the perfect very slow, very
close dance, even if I couldn't technically count it as *Step 5:
Embracing.*

If only this moment would last forever.

Did I just sigh out loud? My eyes popped open, and my back stiffened as I held my breath, listening for his reaction.

"Why'd you tense up?" He pulled his head back a little and looked into my face.

Then I noticed Mom and Mrs. V across the floor, talking near the entrance. I'd forgotten all about Mrs. V! She hugged Mom and headed out the door.

What a rat I was, not to check on her even once.

After six dances with David, with breaks for grazing at the buffet and cutting the wedding cake, I excused myself and zigzagged through the thinning crowd to the ladies room.

Gayle caught up with me. "I had to follow you in here to get a minute with you away from David."

"I'm sorry. Have I ignored you?" Seemed like I tossed everyone else aside because David was there.

"Don't be silly. I wanted to give you some space. But my mother's coming to pick me up, and I have to know—how are things going with him? Other than the obvious, of course." Gayle's eyes opened almost as big and round as the discus she threw in track.

"So … good. It's like we've been close for a long time."

"Great. Now don't get worried thinking about it. Wait and see what happens at school Monday." She hugged me. "'Bye, girl."

"'Bye. Thanks for coming."

The exit door swung closed.

I wiped off the mascara smeared under my eyes and freshened my lipstick. I checked my teeth and popped a breath mint to erase the flavor of crab dip.

Alice poked her head into the ladies room. "Come on, Wendy! They're about to leave!"

Mom and Papa D had changed into casual clothes for their honeymoon. The remaining guests surrounded them, congratulating and wishing them good luck and a safe trip. Alice, Adam, and I parted the crowd to reach our parents.

"I'm so happy for you, Mom." I squeezed her shoulders against mine.

"Thank you, sweetie. I'm happy too, for both of us."

Alice and Adam traded places with me. I reached up and gave Papa D a big hug. "I've decided what I'll call you, if it's okay with you."

"What's that?"

"Papa D."

"I like it." He smiled and kissed my forehead. Then he and Mom climbed inside their limo.

"Have a great time!" Alice and I shouted in unison, with Adam between us. We looked at each other over his head and laughed.

Mom and Papa D waved through the window.

"I love you," Mom mouthed.

"Love you too."

I'd always made fun of people who cried at weddings. I wouldn't do that anymore.

The plan was for the other limo to take Alice, Adam, and me back to the Rends' house, where their next-door neighbor would make sure we got in safely.

"Are you ready?" Alice waited as I dabbed my eyes and nose with a tissue. She held Adam by the hand, dark half-circles rimming below his eyes. His shirt was untucked, missing a button, and stained with punch. White icing dotted his red hair above one ear.

David stood a few yards away with hands in his pockets, his tie loosened.

"I just need a minute." I squeezed Alice's arm and turned in David's direction.

He grinned. "I didn't want to leave without saying good-bye."

"How are you getting home?"

"My brother's coming to pick me up." He swallowed and rubbed the back of his head. "Can I ask you something? In private?"

The clean-up crew scurried about, picking up dirty dishes and moving chairs.

"Sure. Let's go outside." We walked toward the back door. My heart fluttered. Was this going to be it? Step five, maybe even six, a real kiss? My hands grew damp, and I wiped them against my skirt in a pretense of smoothing it.

We sat on a shaded bench under a crape myrtle tree.

"You know I don't drive yet." By his expression, anyone would've thought he faced a firing squad.

"Yeah, I know. Is that what you wanted to tell me?"

He chuckled and shook his head. "No." He wiped sweat from his temple with the heel of his hand.

I waited.

"I was wondering if you'd like to go see a movie sometime, doubling with my brother and his girlfriend."

"Oh! Um, yes. I'll have to get my Mom's permission first, but yes. She'll be back in a week." He didn't say *when*, so shut up, Wendy.

He took a deep breath and smiled like he'd been granted a reprieve.

I couldn't expect anything further from the poor guy.

Steps toward achieving girlfriend status (revised):

5. A date (with hope of an embrace and a kiss.)

Chapter 3

The following Friday was day five of riding the bus to school with Alice—day seven of eating, sleeping, and doing chores in the same house with Alice and Adam. That was a lot of togetherness to get used to all at once.

After school, I left them sorting and packing the remains of their personal stuff and hopped onto my bike. My journey's destination held the possibility of more information about the scandal.

September's afternoon played the trickster, supplying a cool breeze to counteract the sun's warmth on my skin. By the next day the breeze might disappear, leaving behind hot, stagnant air no different from summer.

As I coasted toward Mrs. V's house, I stiffened, commanding myself not to look at my old house next to hers. But I couldn't help it. Like a rejected friend, it slumped on the front lawn waiting for its new owners to claim it and make it feel loved again. The darkened windows drew my attention like big sad eyes.

With a final glance in that direction, I stopped on the driveway behind Mrs. V's car and lowered my kickstand.

A tall sandy-haired boy in baggy shorts stood in the

shaded piece of yard between her house and mine, his back toward me. He faced upward into the oak trees, where a few pairs of squirrels leaped and spiraled through the branches.

That might be Sam, visiting with his father, although Mrs. V hadn't mentioned having any company when I called half an hour earlier. "Hi," I said in a voice meant to be heard but not startle.

He didn't change position or make any move toward acknowledging my presence.

Humph. One of those standoffish guys. I walked right up behind him and tapped his shoulder.

The sandy head turned slowly, followed by the whole lanky body. He grinned like he'd expected someone and wasn't surprised by me at all. Still he said nothing.

"I'm Wendy, a friend of Mrs. Villaturo's." I didn't smile, not wanting him to think I was dying to meet him or anything.

"Hi, I'm Sam." The voice was nasal and unnatural-sounding.

I gasped.

He was deaf.

I'd never had a conversation with a deaf person before, only overheard a little deaf boy speak when I was in elementary school. I'd asked Mom what was wrong with him.

I licked my lips while my mind scrambled for something else to say. Acorns rained down on us.

"They're twice as big as the ones where I live." He

blinked golden-brown eyes that glowed like tiny suns, fringed with the longest lashes I'd ever seen on a boy.

"What?" Could he have misunderstood the few words I'd spoken?

"The squirrels." He pointed into the treetops.

My mouth opened. "Oh-h-h." I peered upward.

"Their tails are much fluffier too."

I faced him so he could see my mouth moving. "Why are squirrels so much smaller in Alaska?" I paced my words and enunciated each one carefully. Then I blushed. He hadn't said where he lived, and now he knew I knew.

"I read lips easily, so just talk to me in a normal way, and I'll understand you." He laughed. "As long as you face me, of course."

I nodded.

"You know where I live?"

"Your grandmother talks about you." Good save.

He returned his attention to the bundles of fur rocketing above our heads. "In Anchorage, the warm season is short, so there's less time to find and store food. Only about a quarter of the squirrels live to adulthood."

"They're so common here, most people think of them as pests." I squinted into the treetops with new appreciation for their hardships. "Why are you so interested in them?"

He shrugged. "I'm interested in all wild animals, really. I volunteer with Alaskan Wildlife Conservation during the summers."

That might explain some of the scabs and scars I'd noticed in his photos—and now. "I like tame animals myself."

"Which ones?"

"Dogs, cats, rabbits, donkeys. Most anything that winds up at animal shelters." I started toward Mrs. V's house and into the sunshine. Sam followed at my side.

"You're the one who got my grandma involved in fostering puppies." He gave me a lopsided grin, squinting one eye.

"That's right." Had Mrs. V talked about me too?

He opened the door and held it for me. "Grandma, Wendy's here."

"Hell-o," I sang out.

As my pupils adjusted to the low light inside, Mrs. V came into view at the kitchen table with Chanceaux at her feet. She sat with her arms resting on the top and stared straight ahead.

Sam grabbed my elbow and stopped me from going into the kitchen, his touch warm but not unpleasant. "She didn't have anything in the house to make for dinner. My dad's at the grocery store."

Oh, no. I turned my face toward Sam's. "She *has* been forgetful lately," I whispered so she wouldn't hear. I didn't know or trust Sam enough to admit more.

He released me, and I went to her.

"Hi, Mrs. V." I spoke in a high voice like I was talking to small child, but I couldn't stop myself. She looked so helpless. I reached out and stroked her hand.

She turned her head toward me. At first, there was no recognition in her eyes, but then she smiled. "Wendy."

"Yes ma'am." I took a deep breath and smiled too. "Told you I'd visit." Had she forgotten we'd talked on the phone less than an hour ago?

"I'm so glad you're here. Let's sit in the living room." She walked to the sofa and turned on a lamp.

The photo albums and mugs of tea remained where we'd left them a week ago. I took the mugs, with mold growing on the surface of the liquid, to the kitchen sink.

"I see you've met Sam," she said when I returned. "It's about time, don't you think?"

"Uh-huh." Why did she make such a big deal about Sam? I picked the old black photo album off the sofa and sat down next to her.

Sam made himself comfortable in the recliner.

The album with Grand-mere and Great-uncle Andre's photo in it was right there in my lap. Mrs. V's mind seemed to be working okay for the moment. It was now or—maybe never.

Sam stared at me, those long-lashed golden eyes unblinking as though he could read my anxiety. The skin on the back of my neck prickled, but I turned to Mrs. V.

"Mrs. V, where's that picture of you and my Grand-mere

Robichaud in Bayou Calmon?" Better if she repeated what she'd said last time about a scandal in my family without my coaxing it out of her. Only then would I be sure whether she'd imagined any of it.

"Oh, yes, Odette and me." She took the album from me and flipped to the page in less than a second. "And there's your great-uncle Andre too."

So far so good. "Why do you suppose I never heard of Grand-mere's brother Andre before? Did he die when he was a kid?"

"No, dear." Her voice softened. "He just disappeared."

Disappeared? That was—crazy. "Why? How?"

"Because of the scandal." She took a deep breath and exhaled. "He fell in love with a girl, and neither family approved." Tears began to fill her eyes.

What had happened to my great-uncle? And how much did Mrs. V know about it? My thoughts ran in a hundred different directions.

A thud sounded outside the front door, and I jerked my head in that direction.

Sam took my cue and rose to his feet. The knob jiggled, and he walked to the door and opened it.

"Sam, help me with the groceries." The deep voice preceded a tall man who stepped through the doorway, arms loaded with bags.

"Gus!" Mrs. V stood up. The photo album slid from her

lap and hit the floor.

My stomach did a bungee.

Tony Villaturo stopped in his tracks and stared into his mother's face.

I groaned. She'd slipped into another time again, back with her dead husband.

Getting this whole story out of Mrs. V was going to take forever. If I got it at all.

Chapter 4

I told Mrs. V good-bye—whether she remembered who I was or not—and Sam walked me out to my bike. His father Tony's grunt when I introduced myself had made it clear he didn't want me there. If only he knew how close Mrs. V and I had become ... but maybe it wouldn't matter to him.

In silence, I grabbed a handlebar and released the kickstand.

Sam touched my shoulder, his fingers lingering just a sec, and it tingled. I took a deep breath, shaking off the electric connection between us, and turned toward him. The deaf must be used to people touching them to get their attention, so they do the same. No big deal.

"Don't worry. Dad plans to take her to the doctor."

If Sam had not been a total stranger until that day, I would've broken down and cried right in front of him. Mrs. V should see a doctor, but I knew in my heart the result wouldn't be good news.

"Thanks." I pressed my lips together and mounted the bike.

This time he placed a hand firmly over mine. "It'll be okay."

I nodded, unable to move, unable to speak. Unshed tears backed up into my throat.

"Will you come back?" His golden sun-eyes gripped my attention.

Was he asking for Mrs. V or for himself? I shook my hand free.

I would be back, of course, even though she had her real family taking over. I'd be there for her just like she'd always been there for me, and nobody could scare me away. Not even Tony.

Sam plunged both hands deep into his pockets and rocked on his heels.

I cleared my throat and found my voice again. "I'll check back sometime next week." Mom and Papa D would return from their honeymoon Sunday, and then Monday we'd move from the Rends' house to the new one.

A smile, starting closed and small, spread open and wide across his teeth. "I'll be here."

I narrowed my eyes to slits. I'd miss a day of school because of the move and would have to play catch up all week. How could he stay here so long? "Don't you have school?"

"My school is pretty good about letting students take educational trips with their parents. And I got my assignments ahead of time."

My eyebrows shot upward. "Educational? You mean coming to wild and mysterious Louisiana? What kind of school is that? Maybe I'd like to switch."

The smile shrunk ever so slightly. "Alaska State School for the Deaf."

I clenched my teeth. *Rats!* Just when I thought Bird Face was gone for good, there she was again, saying something stupid.

My brain wouldn't shut off and let me fall asleep until after midnight. I awoke Saturday morning to a phone ringing somewhere in the house.

Eyes closed, I lifted my head from the pillow for a second. "Alice, would you get that?" I screeched, dropping my head again.

The ringing continued. Where was she? I groaned and rolled out of bed, smacking into Adam, almost knocking him down.

He handed me a receiver from the landline. Sticky with grape jelly. "It's for you."

Oh, good. 'Bout time Mom called to check on us again. Last time was Tuesday, and Alice and I had made a pact not to call our parents on their honeymoon.

"Thanks, little man." I climbed back into bed, phone in hand. "Hello?"

"Hi, Wendy."

I was suddenly wide awake. "David?"

"Yeah. Sorry if I woke you up."

The clock read eight thirty. "Um, that's okay. I had a little trouble getting to sleep last night." I stretched my lips and tongue to get the cotton feeling out of my mouth.

"Well, it's kind of short notice, but could you go with me to see a movie tonight? With my brother and his girlfriend, like I said before."

My heart did a trampoline bounce. "I'd like that." Then I grimaced. "But I haven't had a chance to talk to my mom about it yet. I was hoping she'd call again today."

"Oh." He didn't hide his disappointment.

"Can I call you back this afternoon?"

His voice brightened. "Sure."

I hunted and found a scrap of paper and pen. "What's your number? No caller ID here." I jotted his number down. "How'd you get this number, anyway?"

"You told me you'd be at Alice's, and it's the only Rend listed."

"Oh, yeah. Right." With all the changes of the past week, I'd forgotten I told him.

"I'll talk to you later today then?"

"Definitely. 'Bye, David."

Like the guy said in that movie—the one I wasn't supposed to watch but somebody played at a sleepover—if a boy really wants to reach you, he'll find a way.

Mom called right after lunch. She and Papa D were having

a great time, and she hesitated for only a second in saying yes to my double date with David. She'd met his parents at church and had known them since David and I were in eighth grade, so I wasn't surprised she agreed.

"I just wish I could be there to see you go on your first date. And take a picture of you." Her voice squeaked over island music playing in the background.

Oh no, would she really embarrass me like that? I laughed. "Hopefully, this won't be the last date I have with David."

Shouts and laughter mixed with the music. "I'm having a little trouble hearing you. We'll fly home tomorrow, so you can tell me all about it tomorrow night." A quick good-bye and the call ended.

Knowing Mom, she probably already regretted not giving me a curfew. But as long as she didn't change her mind or embarrass me by calling David's parents …

I punched in David's number as fast as I could and let him know the date was on. I grinned at the happiness in his voice. Unlike with Sam, it was easy to read David's emotions in the sound.

Loading dishes into the dishwasher, I made a mental list of what I had to do to prepare for the date. Wash my hair, tweeze my brows—I needed clean clothes that were nice enough …

Where was Alice? Clarinet music led me to the garage.

"David asked me out!" I yelled.

Alice jerked and spun around, her eyes and mouth open wide. Before she could say anything, I grabbed her arm.

"I need you to help me find something to wear." I forced her to put the clarinet down and follow me back to our room.

"Movie, movie. What to wear to a movie?" Alice pawed through some of my shirts carefully folded in a box.

"I want to look better than I do at school but not like I'm trying too hard." I held a pair of jeans in front of me to check their length. "And I need to feel comfortable."

"This is so 'Wendy.'" She held up a dark blue long-sleeve t-shirt with white braided trim around the neck.

I took it to the mirror and checked the color against my skin. "I never would've thought of this one, but it makes my complexion look good. Brings out the pink in my cheeks. And I like that it's simple."

"Told you." Alice sat down on her bed and folded her arms. She didn't smile.

Something was eating her, and it couldn't be that she had to babysit Adam alone for a few hours. She'd done that for years.

"Alice, this unexpected dating thing—are you okay with it? I mean, you and I just became family, and we're by ourselves until tomorrow night. Am I being a witch to leave you all of a sudden like this?"

"Unh-uh." She shook her head. "It's not like I thought the two of us would start dating at *exactly* the same time."

That was a logical answer, the kind I would've expected her to give. But I remembered how I'd felt when Jennifer's life began to change. Left behind.

I wrapped my arms around Alice's shoulders and hugged her. She loosened her arms and hugged back but stared at the floor.

She had to understand how much this date with David meant to me. She just had to.

Chapter 5

Like a character in a teen spy novel, I'd surveilled the street through a living room window for fifteen minutes. Finally a car turned into the driveway. "They're here."

Alice stared at the TV from the far end of the sofa and didn't move. Adam leapt from his seat and dashed toward the front door with Belle on his heels.

I reached for Adam but snatched a handful of air. "Don't open it," I whispered.

He whirled past me, laughing, and continued to the kitchen. Belle trotted after him.

The doorbell rang. I checked myself in the foyer mirror to make sure my concealer still clung to the zit I'd been trying to dry out all week. That pimple had a half-life longer than most radioactive isotopes (to quote Gayle, such a brainiac). In spite of the zit's attempt to squash my good mood, I had to force myself to relax the grin on my face. I should look happy, not deranged.

On the second ring, I opened the door, knees quaking. They almost gave out beneath me as David appeared under the front porch light.

He was so … shiny. His skin, his hair, his leather jacket—

which was the same warm brown color as his hair—they all glistened in the light. Even his teeth, behind his amazing smile. How could he look so good? So incredibly … perfect.

I became aware that my hand was over my heart. Awkward. I pretended to straighten my necklace and then lowered my arm.

"You look nice." He took in the length of me.

I wanted to say, *Not as good as you* but bit my tongue. "Thank you."

"You're welcome." He poked his head in and obviously spotted Alice's profile across the living room.

I hated that she was being rude. What was wrong with her? "Please come in."

He stepped inside but not enough for me to close the door. "Are you ready? You may need a jacket or something. It's sort of cool tonight."

"I have a sweater right here." I grabbed my big cable cardigan with the tie belt from the back of a nearby chair.

He held the sweater open for me while I worked my arms into it. I wrapped it across my front and tied it closed and then grabbed my shoulder bag from the chair seat.

"'Bye, Alice. I'm leaving."

She gave me a backward wave without turning around. She could at least *pretend* to be happy for me, especially after acting like it was okay for me to go out.

David frowned. "Does she always act like that?"

I sighed. "I don't know what her problem is. Please don't take it personally."

And to think, a week ago I had labeled her personality as mellow. But I'd have to deal with her later. Nothing was going to ruin this night.

Dusk enveloped David and me outside. He darted ahead of me to his brother's car and opened the passenger door. His brother's girlfriend stepped out and said, "Hi," and David moved the front seat forward so I could climb into the back.

I glanced toward the house. A living room curtain fell closed.

"I forgot to ask what time you had to be home." David's buttered-popcorn breath warmed my ear as he leaned toward me in the theater.

A shiver ran down to my toes. "So did I."

"My dad said to have you back before eleven anyway. I can't stay out as late as Ben. We'll have to head home soon after the movie's over."

"That's fine."

I glanced at Ben and his girlfriend, Carla. They seemed like a nice couple. She snuggled against his shoulder, and he murmured into her hair.

Could that be David and me in a couple of years?

The movie started. And I was sitting next to David. *In the dark.* Our arms almost touched. I couldn't think straight.

If someone asked me later what the movie was about, I'd need to say something. Vince Vaughn and Owen Wilson. A combo that was easy to describe, no matter the movie. Good.

The crowd roared with laughter. I'd missed the first funny bit.

Laughing, David grabbed my hand and squeezed it.

He didn't let go.

At 10:45 p.m. David walked me nice and slow toward my front door. Only a couple of details remained to complete *Step 5.*

I swallowed the tiny breath mint I'd popped into my mouth on the ride home. A drum pounded in my chest. I swallowed again and took a deep breath to try to get it under control.

Useless.

The porch light glowed like a spotlight on us. I should've flipped the switch off on my way out. Hopefully, Ben and Carla were paying more attention to each other than to us.

"I had a nice time." Wasn't that what I was supposed to say? It sounded so lame.

David chuckled. "Me too." He reached for my hand that gripped the strap of my bag.

We inched toward each other, and he leaned in.

This is it. This is it. This is it! I held my breath as his face drew near.

His lips. So soft! I closed my eyes, and my free hand found a natural path to his shoulder. His arm wrapped around me.

I could stay like this forever.

Belle met me in the foyer wagging her tail. She nuzzled and licked my hand. Must've been the butter.

I stroked her back. "Thanks for waiting up, girl. I had a really good time," I whispered. At least I had *someone* to talk to who cared. "I think you'll like David."

Belle followed me as I walked on a cloud down the hall and into the room I shared with Alice.

We passed Alice's bed before reaching mine. The absence of her soft, rhythmic breathing told me she was awake. And listening.

Chapter 6

I'd never been so glad to see Mom as when she and Papa D got back on Sunday afternoon.

At the sound of their car pulling into the driveway, Adam shot out of his chair at the kitchen table, still chewing a piece of the roast beef I'd thawed and microwaved for lunch. Next to the kitchen, Alice loaded laundry into the dryer and didn't hear anything—or pretended not to. She hadn't talked to me much since the day before, hadn't asked me anything about my date with David. More than that, she avoided me to the point that Adam had scrunched up one side of his face and blurted, "What's wrong with *her*?"

Responsibility for Adam had scared me before Mom and Papa D left. But I hadn't bargained for responsibility concerning Alice's emotional state, and that was too much to expect of anyone.

"Hey, everybody!" Mom burst through the front door, newly tanned arms extended and eyes sparkling.

Adam reached her first, and I sandwiched him in between Mom and me to give her a big hug.

"You smell like the beach," Adam said.

Mom giggled and kissed the top of his head.

"You look so relaxed." I drew back to see her face. "But I'm glad you're home. I missed you, Mom."

At the sound of the garage door opening, Adam darted away.

"I missed you too. How was your date?" She smiled and squeezed my hand.

"Wonderful. It felt so good to be with David and talk to him away from school." My focus wandered toward Alice slipping out the side door leading to the garage.

If she was giving Mom and me some time alone to catch up, that was nice. If that was the reason.

Mom tossed her tote bag onto the nearest chair. "I'm so happy you had a good time. Will you tell me more about it after I get settled?"

After a private chat with Mom in my room, I lay back on my bed and closed my eyes, thinking of David. I dozed until the aroma of garlic invaded my space. Mom was cooking. I hurried to freshen up and then headed to the kitchen.

"Spaghetti and meatballs! Yum!" I kissed Mom's cheek.

"We're using the dining room tonight. Would you help Alice set the table?" Mom dipped a spoon into the sauce and tasted it.

In the small dining room, Alice rummaged through a buffet cabinet. She looked up when I entered. "Your mom said to do it nice. We have some china in here."

"Okay, how about a tablecloth?"

"Look in that drawer."

I touched her shoulder. "Alice, are we okay?"

She squinted at me and nodded. "Yeah. Of course."

I could count on her being a reasonable person.

I stuffed myself with Mom's meatballs and spaghetti, grateful to have a dinner cooked by someone other than Alice or me. Sure, we'd done all right for a week on mac and cheese, pizza, and turkey sandwiches with avocado. But no way was I ready to live without a parent for longer than that.

"Adam, how did you like having two sisters to look out for you?" Papa D reached over and ruffled Adam's hair.

With a blush, Adam answered by wiggling his shoulders, followed by his whole body.

Papa D laughed. "Looks like you girls did a good job."

Mom raised her glass of water. "Here's to our new family."

I tested a smile on Alice, and she smiled back. We raised our glasses.

After the stress of the past nine days, it would've been nice to lie around on Monday. But if my new family and I hadn't been moving into our new house, I would've been in school anyway.

I'd hauled stuff off the rental truck since 7:00 a.m. and finally took a mid-morning break on the front steps to drink a bottle of water. If anyone asked me again "Where does this go?" I might scream. My feet hurt like crazy. And I stank.

After this, I never wanted to move to another house again—ever. Unless it was with David.

Oh, well. One more stretch and then I needed to get up and start unpacking. I pointed my toes and raised both arms over my head.

"Dad! What are you doing here?"

A big grin spread across his face. He strolled up the sidewalk holding a gift bag in front of him.

I scrambled to my feet and gave him a hug.

"It's gotten so hard to keep up with you, I thought I'd better give you one of your Christmas presents early."

I gasped and snatched the bag and then tore into the tissue paper inside. "A smart phone! Aiyeeeeeee!"

Dad chuckled at my Cajun exclamation.

I kissed his cheek. "Thank you, thank you, Dad."

"You're welcome. How've you been? I haven't talked to you in a couple of weeks."

I used my singsong voice and shifted my shoulders back and forth. "I went on a date Sa-tur-day."

He raised his eyebrows. "Wow, really?"

What kind of reaction was that? But I forged ahead. "With David. You remember him. The boy who played the lead in

Oklahoma! at the spring program last year."

"I'm not sure—"

Mom stepped out onto the porch, with Papa D right behind her. "Hi, Pete. How are you? You remember Daniel."

Dad blinked and turned from me to them. "Hi, Cathy. I'm doing just fine." He produced the kind of smile you use when you hate the new sweater someone gives you for Christmas. "Congratulations to both of you." Dad offered his hand to Papa D, and they shook.

My eyes met Mom's. She must've felt the strangeness of the moment, too. But like pulling a Band-Aid off a healing wound, it was better to get this new family situation out in the open air right away for everyone to get used to. She crossed her arms over her middle. Maybe her insides flipped, same as mine did.

Dad placed a hand on my shoulder, as if renewing his claim on me as *his* daughter. "There's something I want to invite Wendy to do, and I may as well let you know about it at the same time."

I grimaced. What Dad sometimes thought was a great outing often wasn't. *Circus, anyone?* And no surprise could possibly be as good as the phone.

"Why don't we sit down?" Mom started for a bench and chairs along the porch wall.

I took the opportunity to sit again, choosing the bench. "What is it, Dad?"

"I'm taking Margaret to meet the rest of the family that didn't make it to our wedding. Aunt Renee and her kids, if you remember them. I'd like you to come with us—to Bayou Calmon."

My eyes opened wide. *The scandal.* What luck!

Dad frowned, so I smiled to assure him the invitation wasn't a bad thing.

"Do you want to go?" Mom and Dad asked at the same time.

"Yeah, I do. But when?" I focused on Dad and held my breath. Please, not this weekend, not this weekend.

"This coming weekend. We'll spend Saturday night there."

I puffed my cheeks and blew out. That figured. Trying to make up to Alice for ditching her to go out with David, I'd promised to spend the weekend helping to repaint her room. But if she were willing …

"Can Alice go with me?" I blurted.

Dad opened his mouth, shut it, and then opened it again. "I don't see why not. Your stepbrothers are going fishing with their grandparents, so there's room in the car."

Mom raised her eyes to Papa D's. "If she'd like to, I'm fine with it," he said.

I'd have to explain to Alice why I was itching to go to Bayou Calmon—and get her to play along without Mom or Dad figuring out my ulterior motive. But if anyone could appreciate a good mystery, it should be my new sister, the mysterious sticky-note writer of my past.

"This is a little different from trying to figure out who left you a note." Alice scrunched her nose as she sat cross-legged against the headboard of her bed.

"I know that." Why was she being so difficult? I plopped onto the foot of the bed. "But this is my great uncle who simply *vanished*. Wouldn't you want to know what happened if one of your family members disappeared?"

Oh, no. I didn't mean her mother dying. I gritted my teeth. She studied the pattern on her comforter.

"Alice, this is my only chance. Mrs. V can hardly remember her own family, much less give me details about mine. And my Dad may not be willing to talk."

"Do you even have any idea where to start? I picture us running around and not getting anything accomplished." She scowled and shook her head.

"It's the only place I *can* start. And how else would I travel to Bayou Calmon? Even if I drove there by myself someday, Dad's relatives might not be willing to open up unless my dad is with me."

"But you promised we'd spend the whole weekend together, just the two of us. At *home*. We're sisters now, but we don't spend any more time alone together than we did before."

Wrinkles formed between her strawberry blonde eyebrows.

My heart softened to a marshmallow. She'd been the only female in her house for years, and she was hanging onto me like a life raft. "I know, and I'm sorry it hasn't worked out yet, but it will."

"I'd like to be with you, but there?" She shrugged. "Maybe I should just stay here."

"I could really use your help, Alice." I stuck out my lower lip.

She narrowed her eyes. A low growl started in her throat. She reached for a pillow.

I covered my head.

"Arrrgh!" She laughed and whacked me hard.

I slid off the bed, and my butt hit the wood floor. "Ow!"

We both laughed until our sides hurt. I hiccupped, and we started laughing again.

As we lay gasping for breath, Alice said, "What does 'Calmon' mean, anyway?"

I hiccupped again. "Alligator."

Her blue eyes opened wide, their pupils shrinking to tiny black dots.

"Prepare yourself. You'll see your first one in five days."

Chapter 7

The next morning, Alice and I got up twenty minutes earlier to catch the school bus for the first time from our new house. And we arrived ten minutes earlier than before. Alice got in a little extra clarinet practice before class. I got more time with David.

He entered my new number into his phone. I sneaked a study of his profile while he worked.

Sigh.

Steps toward achieving girlfriend status:

6. Saved on speed-dial (Check.)

He looked up and grinned. "So, what will you do in Bayou Calmon?"

I didn't expect any questions. How much should I tell him? His green eyes encouraged me to trust. I took a deep breath and exhaled. "Look for a missing person."

He laughed. "Seriously? Who?"

"My great uncle. There was some kind of scandal about him being in love with the wrong girl. Then he disappeared. I want to know what happened to him."

"How did you find out about this?" He returned his phone to his shirt pocket.

"My old next door neighbor, Mrs. Villaturo, had a photo of herself with my Grand-mere Robichaud in Bayou Calmon. There was a boy in the background and Mrs. V said he was my Grand-mere's brother. But I'd never heard she had one."

"What do you think happened to him?"

"I don't know. Mrs. V was about to cry when I asked about him again. But she isn't behaving like herself. She's forgetful and imagines things. She even thought she saw her dead husband. And now her son is at her house, so it's almost impossible to get any more information."

"Can't you ask your dad?"

"I might try, but my mom acted like he won't be willing to talk about it. Maybe once he and I are in Bayou Calmon, he'll open up. Except—my stepmother Margaret will be with us."

David shrugged. "The guy could've left home just because he wanted to."

"Possibly. But why all the mystery? I may have to do some digging."

"You wouldn't do anything to put yourself in danger, would you?" He raised his eyebrows until ridges formed across his forehead.

Awww. He was worried about me. "Not on purpose." I grinned.

He rubbed the back of his head. "Where is this place exactly?"

"Southwest from here, somewhere deep in Cajun country.

It's so rural they don't have their own post office. The funniest thing will be seeing how my stepmother Margaret reacts to the place."

He sighed. "So I guess we won't see each other this weekend." He stroked the hair falling down my back, and I melted.

"I guess not." I looked deep into pools of green.

His voice softened. "I'm glad you told me about this."

"Me, too." I smiled. It filled my chest with warmth to talk to David about something I couldn't share with anyone else other than my sister.

But I didn't tell him about my new friendship with Sam.

By the end of homeroom, everyone who knew David and me seemed aware that we'd gone out on Saturday and were now a couple.

Each time we ran into each other and stopped to chat for a minute, people stared and whispered—and sometimes smiled. It was nice to receive stares of the admiring kind. Most of the ones I'd received before this year had been anything but.

When David's jock buddies met him in the halls, they poked him in the ribs or slapped him on the back. Why did guys do that? So immature. But I guess it meant something good as far as their opinion of me was concerned.

At lunchtime, heads turned as David joined me at the table with Alice and Gayle. I was so proud to be his girlfriend.

"Ladies." He tipped an imaginary hat to them.

Gayle and I chuckled. I loved his sense of humor.

Alice remained quiet, keeping her head down and chewing like a grazing bovine. Really? Was she still mad? We'd straightened things out about spending more time together, or so I'd thought. Maybe she was jealous after all, although she wouldn't admit it. Short of finding her a boyfriend, I didn't know what to do to make her feel better about David and me.

In spite of talking to Gayle on the phone Sunday, she grilled me all day, every chance she got, for details about *everything* concerning the date. But I held the memory close to me, protecting it, and shared only a few things to satisfy her curiosity.

Jennifer caught me in English class, squeezed my hand, and said she was happy for me. She wouldn't lie.

A few other girls plastered on fake smiles and said things like "Awesome" and "Congratulations." Congratulations? Was there a contest?

Only one girl looked like she was about to cry.

Tookie.

Chapter 8

Don't most people get to take it easy on Friday afternoons?

Once again I got home from school, ate a quick snack with Belle, and then jumped on my bike and raced over to Mrs. V's house.

No calling first. She didn't remember my call last time, and I wasn't about to give Tony the chance to tell me no.

Out of breath, I coasted onto the driveway. Only Mrs. V's car. Good.

Sam gave a single wave from a folding aluminum lawn chair under a tree, where he scribbled in a notebook.

I smiled and waved back.

He continued in the notebook. Not the warmest reception.

I shook off the needling disappointment, irritated with myself. What did I expect?

"I knew you'd come today." He remained seated and only glanced at me as I parked the bike.

Presumptuous *and* rude. David would've at least gotten up and said he was glad to see me. Even before he started becoming my boyfriend.

"Yeah, well, I'm worried about Mrs. V." I walked straight

toward him. He wasn't going to ignore me, if that's what he had in mind.

Surprise. He rose and fetched another lawn chair that leaned against the backside of the tree. That was nice. He found a level spot and set up the chair next to his.

His notebook lay open on his chair seat. Pencil drawings of squirrels.

An artist *and* animal advocate. Gotta love that. I picked up the notebook and flipped to more sketches on the next page. "Hey, these are good."

"Thanks." He extended his hand for the notebook, and I handed it over. "Just passing the time."

"I draw too."

"I know."

I cocked an eyebrow. No secrets kept around here. Hope I didn't tell Mrs. V anything over the years I didn't want repeated. Well, it was ridiculous to worry now, considering.

"Did Mrs. V go to the doctor?"

"Yeah. Before we go in, I'll tell you what the doctor said." Unlike the speech of most people, his held no inflection I could interpret.

"Okay."

"Maybe you should sit down."

Hope sank. I sat.

He dove in, his golden eyes never leaving my face. "She has Alzheimer's."

My worst fear for her, and my insides trembled.

"Do you know what that is?"

I hung my head and spoke through fingers covering my mouth. "I've heard of it." She was losing her memory. How long before she would forget me completely?

He pulled my hand away from my mouth. "What?"

"I'm sorry. I forgot you needed to read my lips. Yes, I know what Alzheimer's is. It affects her memory."

"But it's more than that. It affects all her mental ability and eventually the physical."

"Isn't there anything she can take for it?"

"She has meds now to try to slow it down."

I took a deep breath. "Will she be okay for a while longer?"

He looked at the ground for a minute and then at me again. "The thing is, my dad doesn't want her to live by herself."

"She could go into a nursing home." My heartbeat grew rapid.

He nodded.

"There's a great one here. It looks very nice." The pitch of my voice rose to that of a pleading child. "And I could still visit her every week." I grappled for fragments to support my argument. "I would. Really, I would."

"If my dad decides to let her stay in Louisiana."

"No!" I jumped out of my chair, and it collapsed with a

clatter.

"Wendy, I'm sorry."

"I don't believe you. You and your dad just want to do what's easy for you."

She couldn't leave. I'd rather have her not recognize me than not have her at all.

I sprinted to her front door and burst in.

"Wendy, are you okay?" She remembered me! "Whatever is wrong?"

I sobbed into her shoulder, and she hugged me tight. She smelled of vanilla and jasmine.

"Mrs. V, I love you so much."

She sighed. "I guess Sam told you I have Alzheimer's."

I wiped my eyes with my hands. "I would've insisted if he hadn't told me."

"You know it will get worse with time." She spoke almost in a whisper, as if she was breaking bad news about me instead of about herself.

I nodded.

She took my shoulders and held me at arm's length, looking into my eyes. "We'll always be close, even if we don't live near each other."

Was she referring to the local nursing home—or Alaska? I kissed her cheek. "I would never forget you."

What else could I say? I was an outsider, and I was losing her—a little piece at a time right now and possibly altogether very soon.

Sam had turned his chair so he was able to see me exit the house. He stood up and put his sketchbook and pencil on the seat.

I straightened my shoulders, lifted my chin, and stomped toward him.

"Look, I know this isn't your decision to make. It's your dad's. But I love her too, and I just hope your dad will give the medicine some time to work before—"

"I know. I hope so too. But somebody needs to be near her all the time to start taking care of her soon."

I opened my mouth to argue again.

"And I do miss her."

I shut my trap. Of course he did. She was *his* long before she was mine. A jealous pang struck me.

"Are we friends?" He dipped his head and smiled.

I double-blinked. "Are we?"

"I think so."

A strange beginning for a friendship, but I was just getting used to making new friends. Who was I to judge the correctness of it?

He stuck his hands into his pockets and stretched his lips into a closed smile.

I took a deep breath and flipped my hair off one shoulder

with my hand. "Look, I'm going out of town this weekend, but I have a smart phone now. Do you want to exchange e-mail addresses?" Only David deserved my number.

He nodded.

"Good. If you would, please let me know how she's doing." I wrote my address on the back of his sketchpad.

He tore off a corner of a page and wrote his.

I stuck it in my pocket.

"You could let me know how you're doing too." He wrinkled his nose and squinted that squinty hawk eye again.

His voice sounded almost normal. Or maybe I was getting used to it.

Chapter 9

At the crack of dawn, Alice and I sprawled in the backseat of Dad and Margaret's slow-moving land barge—a brand new Chevy Suburban—on our way to Bayou Calmon. The smell of leather seats filled my nostrils.

Already, I'd made progress in making up with Alice simply by having her there with me. She started smiling as soon as everyone loaded into the car and didn't quit for miles. She bombarded Dad with questions about everything we passed along the way—oil derricks and refinery tanks, rice and sugar cane fields, seafood-packing plants. You'd think she'd never taken a road trip before.

About an hour into the trip, Dad smiled at her in his rearview mirror. "Alice, you're not from Louisiana, are you?"

That cracked me up.

Alice blushed. "No, sir."

I reached over and hugged her as well as I could with our seatbelts on. "Someday, I'll take you to tour one of those old plantation homes. How about The Myrtles? They say it's haunted."

"Ooh, definitely. I visited some haunted castles in Europe. They were awesome."

We settled back again and talked about music and school, and everything was fine between us.

Another hour and a half later, we'd just turned onto an uneven blacktop road when I received a text.

David.

Alice heaved an exaggerated sigh, making me aware of a huge grin on my face. I immediately deleted it. The grin, not the text.

HEY, ARE YOU THERE YET?

I cut Arnold Schwarzenegger eyes toward Alice, who looked out the window. I needed to push Papa D to buy Alice a phone for Christmas. Then maybe some of her musician buddies would keep her busy once in a while.

ALMOST. IT LOOKS LIKE A SCENE FROM A SWAMP MONSTER MOVIE. WHAT ARE YOU UP TO?

NOT MUCH. CLEANING LEAVES OFF THE PATIO.

EXCITING.

HOPE WE CAN GO OUT AGAIN SOON.

ME TOO.

The corners of my lips curled.

Steps toward achieving girlfriend status:

7. Being missed (Check.)

"This is it." Dad slowed the land barge on the gravel driveway for some loose chickens that clucked and squawked but finally got out of the way. We rolled up to the gray cypress-wood house I remembered from childhood—shrunk to only a cottage—nestled under the oak trees with Spanish moss hanging from their branches. The covered porch I used to play on with my cousin Jerome extended across the entire front of the house with an outside set of stairs leading to sleeping areas above the ceiling. Two old rocking chairs remained on the porch, needing a paint job just like before. A scruffy yellow tabby cat slept in one. He was new.

"Are we staying here?" Alice's face had gone white, like she was going to be sick.

"Don't worry. We won't." Margaret couldn't have said it any sooner. "We'll sleep at a hotel." Margaret gave Dad a look that meant business.

Alice and I exhaled simultaneously.

"Hey, glad y'all could make it." Aunt Renee pushed open the screen door and stepped out onto the porch. She'd become an older version of Dad with graying hair, wearing a faded man-shirt and equally faded jeans.

Dad got out of the car, grinning. "Hey, sis. Great to see you." He went around to Margaret's side and opened her door. "This is my wife, Margaret."

Margaret smiled and got out. "Hello." Then she reached back in for her designer handbag. With her coordinated pants outfit and stylish hair, she looked like a wealthy city girl in Aunt Renee's simple surroundings.

Aunt Renee's battered old car was parked next to the house. A tender spot pinged in my heart. Aunt Renee was poor—a poor that had been invisible to me as a kid. It couldn't have been easy for her to send a Christmas gift to me every year.

"It's nice to finally meet you, Margaret. Welcome to Bayou Calmon. Sorry I couldn't make your wedding." She slapped her thigh. "Had knee surgery. Still not right after all this time." Her gait was less than smooth as she moved closer to the edge of the porch.

"I understand, and there's no need to apologize. It's nice to finally meet you too." Margaret climbed the porch steps with Dad.

"And is that Wendy?" Aunt Renee's face lit up as I got out of the car.

"Yeah, it's me, Aunt Renee."

"I haven't seen you since you were this high." She held her palm three feet above and parallel to the porch.

I trotted onto the porch and into her open arms.

Alice followed me up.

"Who's this?" Aunt Renee released me and smiled at Alice.

"My friend Alice."

She elbowed me.

"I mean, my *sister* Alice."

"I'm glad you could come too, Alice." Aunt Renee held the screen door open. "Ya'll come on in and have some iced tea. Lunch is almost ready, and I'll get Jerome and Mattie to help you with the bags when they get home. Then we can talk about what you'd like for supper."

Margaret pinched Dad's arm.

"Thanks, but no need, Renee. We'll treat you all to dinner at our hotel this evening." Dad settled that.

We trooped into the house. I checked my e-mail on the way. One from Sam.

GRANDMA IS HAVING A NICE TIME. SHE STILL REMEMBERS HOW TO PLAY SCRABBLE.

Thank you, God.

I held onto the phone but claimed a glass of Aunt Renee's sweet tea. "Alice, let's go out back."

She stuck close behind me, tea in hand.

More rockers waited on the smaller back porch facing the bayou. The whole house rested on pilings only yards from the murky, sluggish water, which could rise much higher and very quickly during a rainy period.

Alice and I each took a seat. Every animal and insect on the bayou seemed to come alive at our presence—splashing, squawking, clicking, and rustling the leaves.

"I thought it would be really quiet here, like in the movies." Alice scoped out the scenery along the water's edge—long-legged birds, wild plants, and crawly things on the damp earth.

I grinned. "Sometimes."

Alice turned her face upward into the treetops just as a big black snake writhed and dropped into the water. "Eeeee!" She jerked, sloshing tea on her arm. She whipped her head and scanned the area around the porch like she expected an army of snakes to invade us.

I laughed. "It's okay, Alice. They usually don't come onto the porch unless the water gets high. And we'll stay out from under the trees."

She exhaled, her eyes big and round, and wiped away the tea with her other hand.

E-mail alert. Sam again.

SEEN ANY WILD ANIMALS?

Ha! I started to e-mail Sam back when a wooden pirogue glided toward us on the water. A small and simple boat, it was meant for one adult. A dark-haired teenage boy wearing a faded LSU t-shirt manned the paddle. A young dark-haired girl sat in front.

The boy banked the pirogue, and he and the girl climbed out.

Jerome and Mattie! I jumped to my feet. Jerome was a year or two older than me, and last time I'd seen him, just a skinny kid. Mattie had been a toddler.

"Hey, cousin!" He said it like a Cajun: coo-za. With tanned muscular arms, he pulled the pirogue farther up on dry land and wiped his hands on his jeans.

"Hey, Jerome!" We met each other half way, and he squeezed me in a big hug, lifting me off the ground.

After he set me down, I turned to Mattie. Her hair in a ragged ponytail, she wore cut-off jean shorts and a sweatshirt. She must've been ten or eleven years old.

"Hi, Mattie." Because she couldn't have remembered me, I smiled without touching her.

"Hi." Her lips formed a tiny, curved smile. She sidled up close to her brother.

Was I ever that shy?

"It's okay, Mattie. This is Wendy. You just haven't seen each other in a long time."

"And this is Alice, my ... new sister." I jerked my thumb to indicate Alice, who stood in front of her rocker on the porch.

"Nice to meet you, Alice." Jerome's dark eyes locked with Alice's blue ones.

Her cheeks flushed a bright pink—and the look on her face! Embarrassing.

"So, how ya been, Jerome?" I rushed to cover the awkward moment.

He tore his eyes away from Alice. "Fine, just fine. Hang on. I left something in the pirogue." He trotted back toward the bank.

Alice's eyes got big, and she pressed fingers against her lips to contain a smile. Grinning, I climbed back on the porch and patted her shoulder.

"Pecans." Jerome held a burlap sack, the contents clacking like little wooden balls. "Our neighbor sells 'em."

He and Mattie moved toward the house.

"Hope Mama's got lunch almost ready. I'm starved."
Jerome opened the screen door with one arm, the sack of
pecans over his other shoulder.

After what Aunt Renee called a "light" lunch—andouille
sausage jambalaya—Jerome, Mattie, Alice, and I left the
grownups indulging in black Cajun coffee you could stand a
stick in and went out back again.

I took a rocker seat to e-mail Sam.

Jerome walked to the edge of the bayou and stood for a
minute. "Hey, Alice, come here a second. I want to show you
something."

Alice looked at me.

I shrugged.

She headed toward Jerome.

He pointed at the water. "See that gator over there?"

Alice took a step back. "Yeah."

Jerome grabbed her by the arms and pretended he was
going to throw her into the water.

"No!" Alice screamed so loud a crane took flight.

I rushed to the water and took a photo before the gator
swam past.

By the time I e-mailed the image to Sam, Alice and
Jerome were hanging onto each other laughing.

After a fried shrimp dinner at the hotel that evening—

surprisingly luxurious accommodations outside Bayou Calmon—Jerome, Alice, Mattie, and I headed to the pool area. Jerome looked extra handsome in a button-down shirt and khakis, and Alice was positively stunning in a skirt and pullover top.

Mattie and I looked good too, but who cared? I wore a sleeveless red dress with a matching cardigan. Mattie wore a blue dress and had tied a blue satin ribbon across the top of her hair like a headband. I told her she was pretty. I always wished for someone to tell me that at her age.

All four of us plopped onto some lounge chairs and put our feet up as the sun began to set. Jerome placed his hands behind his head and closed his eyes. Alice fixed her gaze on him. Thank goodness he couldn't see her.

I patted my chair for Mattie to join me, and she snuggled in. I stroked the hair spilling over her shoulders, just like Mom used to do mine when we sat together.

This side of Dad's family was so sweet. It would be awful if something bad had happened to one of them. I prayed Great-uncle Andre was alive and safe, or if dead, had lived a long and happy life. But how could I bring up the subject to find out? I glanced at Jerome resting peacefully.

Hmmm. Jerome's dad had left Aunt Renee a long time ago, but he'd been blond, if I remembered right. Jerome had the same dark good looks as Andre did in the old photograph. "Jerome, do you favor anyone in the family?" Blunt, but what else is new?

Jerome's eyes popped open. He turned his head toward me and paused before speaking. "Yeah. Mama said I look like our great-uncle."

"Who?"

"Andre. He's gone now, disappeared, dead probably. I don't know." He closed his eyes again. Conversation over.

Sparks fired in my brain. Jerome had heard something about Andre too!

Alice's gaze on Jerome remained steady. Didn't she pay attention to what he said?

Guess not. She was supposed to help me solve the mystery, but it looked like I'd have to figure out what happened to him on my own.

So now what?

Tomorrow was Sunday, and Dad had already said we'd head home early. Probably Margaret's idea. No time for research at the local library or newspaper—if Bayou Calmon had one. If any other family members still existed who might know something, they were such distant relatives that Dad had never mentioned them. Maybe I'd try to get Aunt Renee alone and question her.

Mattie squeezed my hand. "*I* know," she whispered in my ear.

I double-blinked and looked down at her upturned face. Mattie? What could she know?

"Mattie, do you—" I began in as low a whisper as possible.

Dad blasted through the nearest door. "Let's go, y'all. Renee's ready to go home."

We all rode in the Suburban to return Aunt Renee, Jerome, and Mattie home, sitting too close together for questions. Not too close for Alice and Jerome, though, who entwined their fingers when they thought no one was looking.

I sighed. Only a small window of opportunity remained to get some answers about Andre before departure the next day.

Getting undressed for bed at the hotel, I tried to interpret what Mattie may have hinted at knowing. The reason he disappeared? Whether or not he was dead? Or—I shuddered—how he died?

I would try to talk to her out of earshot of the rest of the family when we stopped to say good-bye in the morning. I climbed into my bed, my phone in hand.

Alice had a smile plastered on her face as she lay in the other bed reading a gossip magazine. She didn't roll her eyes or anything when my phone rang and I answered saying, "Hi, David."

"How are things going so far?" He yawned audibly and laughed. "Excuse me."

"It's not as boring as all that, but I haven't found out anything except that Great-uncle Andre did exist. Whether he still does, I don't know."

"What about digging some more tomorrow?"

"I'll do my best, but we're leaving pretty early."

"Can't say I'm sad about that. The sooner you leave, the sooner you'll be back."

Heart flutter. "I'll call and fill you in on everything after I get home, okay?"

"Sounds good. 'Night, Wendy."

"'Night, David."

Smiling, I reached to turn the lamp off just as an e-mail alert sounded.

No message. Only a drawing of the alligator I'd photographed and sent to Sam earlier. He'd signed it in the corner. "Sam Villaturo."

I smiled. I wanted that drawing.

Margaret couldn't get out of Cajun country soon enough. She knocked on our hotel room door at six forty five to wake Alice and me. "Let's get packing."

After eating a big breakfast and checking out of the hotel, we traveled again to Aunt Renee's.

Once there, we exchanged hugs and kisses all around, although Jerome and Alice disappeared for a few minutes somewhere in the middle. I didn't have the chance to get Aunt Renee or Mattie alone for any questions. Dad monopolized their time reminiscing with long-winded accounts of old family

Cynthia T. Toney

get-togethers. Margaret had to sit and wait. I sympathized with her, having heard the boring stories more times than I could count.

I strolled around the yard until Dad announced it was time to go.

Alice and I found each other outside.

"Look." Smiling, she held a slip of paper with Jerome's phone number on it. "I gave him our home number."

"That's great," I whispered, squeezing her hand.

Jerome walked up to Alice, so I left them and climbed into the car.

While I strapped into my seatbelt, Mattie appeared at my window. I opened the door.

"This is for you." She smiled and handed me a small package wrapped in white paper and tied with a ribbon—her blue hair ribbon.

I gasped. "Thank you, Mattie. You're so sweet."

"You'll like it." She leaned in and kissed me on the cheek.

"Is it something you made?"

"It's something I found. In our tool shed." She placed an index finger to her lips.

I mimicked her action and hastily slipped the bundle into my shoulder bag, just as Alice opened her side of the car.

Nothing had better crawl out of that package when I opened it.

Chapter 10

What a sorry investigator I turned out to be.

Too timid to pry, I was no Sammy Keyes or Nancy Drew, that's for sure. But in my defense, I'd spent only twenty-four hours in Bayou Calmon, not enough time to bring up the subject of Andre in casual conversation or do any hard investigating either. And this situation called for discretion. Just talking about it had made Mrs. V cry. I'd never seen her do that before and never wanted to see it again.

The Internet was the next logical place to search for information. If Andre's disappearance created news, there should be a record of it somewhere.

Satisfied with my new plan, I leaned my head against the back of the seat and closed my eyes. Alice already dozed, snoring softly. The land barge mixed its low rumble with the soft music playing from Dad's sound system.

The next thing I knew, we were back at our house.

My overnight bag unloaded from the trunk, I couldn't wait to call David.

I locked my bedroom door, glad to have my own space again, and Belle jumped onto the bed with me.

"Hello," David answered, his voice like melted milk chocolate.

"Hey, I'm back."

He laughed. "Did you sleep in the car?"

"You can tell?"

"Of course. You sound like you did the first time I called you."

"I'm not going to act embarrassed."

"You shouldn't."

"I won't."

"So what did you find out?"

"Nothing, really. My cousin Jerome said he looks like Great-uncle Andre, according to my aunt."

"All right. What next?"

"Internet search, maybe later today."

"Sounds good."

Tiny pause. Should I let him know I missed him? "Sorry I didn't get to see you at church this morning."

"Your loss. I looked very dapper."

I snorted. "Have you been reading fashion magazines again?"

"Next week, I'll go for spiffy."

"You know, we might be changing churches because of the move."

"I hope not."

"Me, too."

"My parents don't remember much about you. I said I'd re-introduce you to them next time I see you there."

Officially meeting the parents? Yay!

Steps toward achieving girlfriend status:

8. Meeting the parents.

"I'll try to attend one more time."

"Good. Sorry, but I've gotta go help Ben wash his car. Riding with him isn't free."

I laughed. "Okay. I'll see you at school tomorrow. 'Bye."

"'Bye."

I set my phone on the nightstand next to my shoulder bag. Oh yeah, Mattie's gift! I pulled it out. "Isn't this exciting, Belle? Just like Christmas."

She sniffed the package. If anything crawled out, Belle would catch it.

I untied Mattie's pretty ribbon and set it aside. She may not have many girlie things like that. I should mail it back to her, along with a thank you note. No matter what the gift.

The white paper, double-wrapped around its contents, opened easily at the taped seams.

My eyes grew wide.

Inside lay a stack of small pink envelopes, slit open at the tops. Letters, half a dozen or so. Each of them addressed to Andre Broussard. From the mystery girl?

My heart pattered and my scalp tingled. Thank you, Mattie! Good find in the tool shed, little cousin.

The handwritten mailing address was Kentucky, the return address Bayou Calmon. The postmarks ranged from 1960 through 1961, where the dates were legible. Mattie appeared to have arranged them in chronological order as best she could.

With shaky hands, I withdrew the contents of the first and oldest envelope. Sheets of pink paper.

My dear Andre,

I was relieved and thankful to receive your letter telling me you'd arrived safely in Kentucky and had found a good job there. At the same time, I'm frightened for you. I will pray every day for God to keep you safe in the coal mines.

Please forgive my behavior when we said good-bye. I do understand why you needed to get away from Bayou Calmon and have some time to think about what to do. But also please understand that from my point of view, it seems you wanted to get away from me as well.

After some time has passed and the anger in both our families has subsided, I may be able to travel north by train on the pretext of visiting my cousin in Illinois. She lives across the state line from western Kentucky.

Whomp, whomp! My door rattled. "Wendy, food!" Adam shouted.

Rats! Just when I was getting started. I glanced at my

watch. Two o'clock. No wonder my stomach growled. "Okay, I'm coming," I yelled through the closed door.

I stuffed the letter under my pillow, gathered all the envelopes, and shoved them under my bed.

Take-out fried chicken with mashed potatoes and gravy really hit the spot.

I picked up my plate and glass to carry them to the sink.

Mom placed a hand on my arm. "Hold on, Wendy, Daniel and I think this would be a good time for a meeting with you girls."

"A meeting?" I sat down again.

"Adam, you're excused," Papa D said.

Were we in trouble? I caught Alice's eye.

She raised her eyebrows and shrugged.

Mom cleared her throat. "A lot of new things have happened all at once, and Daniel and I only recently have had a chance to discuss them. One thing involves you two."

Papa D took over. "It concerns the issue of dating."

No! Heat rose up my neck, and I shot Mom an incredulous look, my jaw dropping. "You gave me permission, Mom."

"I know, and I apologize. You and I never talked about a definite age you'd be allowed to start dating. I was on my honeymoon and wasn't thinking, that with Daniel and me having two daughters now, we should treat you both the same."

My mouth still hanging open, I turned to Papa D.

"You see, Wendy, I'd always told Alice she couldn't date until she was fifteen. And she's been okay with that, haven't you, Alice?"

Alice turned every shade of red that exists but nodded without looking at me.

"Of course she was okay with it—nobody asked her out." I regretted the words as soon as I said them.

Alice's face scrunched up like I'd stuck her with a pencil. Ugh. Call me a jerk.

"Wendy." Mom looked to heaven, sighed, and set a steely gaze on me. "You should be ashamed of yourself."

"I'm sorry, but that's about to change anyway. Tell them, Alice."

Alice frowned and wiggled her head rapidly from side to side.

What a wimp. I held up both palms. "Okay, I'll say it, then. Alice has a crush on my cousin Jerome. They already exchanged phone numbers. What if he calls and wants to drive over here and take her out?" I jutted my chin and looked both adults squarely in the eyes, challenging them.

"How could you, Wendy?" Alice's glare firing like blue lasers, she shoved back from the table. "I'll never tell you anything again!" She jumped out of her chair and fled the room. The wall stopped the chair from toppling over.

Papa D watched Alice go, his face as red as hers. Then he stood and placed both palms on the table, his lips set in a grim line. "Let's just deal with facts here, not supposition. We want to lay out some dating rules that both of you can follow—starting now."

Mom clasped her hands together. "I agree."

My cheeks burned. How could she take his side? "But I've already gone out on a date. I'll look like an idiot if I tell David I can't go out with him again until I turn fifteen. That's not until summer!"

"We've thought of that," Mom said. "So we decided that you can go out with David for one evening every other weekend, if we approve of who's doing the driving and you get home before eleven."

My head felt about to explode. "Every other weekend?" I shoved my chair back too, tears beginning to flow. "I hope you don't mind if I leave and go to my room, since you think Alice and I should act the same." I stormed out.

Belle nuzzled my hand as I lay face down on my bed, safe behind my closed door.

I hadn't been this mad since the night of the spring program last year when I blew up at Dad for not letting me know whether he'd be there. If I expected anyone to be tough about dating, it would be him, my *real* father. Instead, I had *those* two ganging up on me. And Alice sure was quick to tell me how to be a sister, but when I needed her support, she just sat there like a dope.

Stepfamily. Blended? Hmph!

I swung my arm over Belle, buried my face in her fluffy coat, and inhaled its earthy smell until the anger began to drain out of me.

Stretching, I righted myself and then scooted backward to the headboard. I may as well watch a little mind-numbing TV and try to forget about this disastrous situation. Mom would soon come to her senses and change her mind. Surely she would.

I fluffed the pillows behind me. One pillow crackled. The letter. A blind search with one hand produced it.

Blah, blah—yeah, that's where I left off.

I'm so very sad that we can't be together, at least not for now. Maybe one day our families will understand.

Tell me about it, sister.

In the meantime, I'll do everything I can to see you again, as I hope you will try your best to see me.

My father and mother, aunties, and even my sister and brother pat my shoulder or my hand and say things like "You'll get over him and find someone right for you," when I know that you're the right one for me. Or, "You'll forget; life moves on," but I feel my life has stopped now that you're gone. I know they're trying to make me feel better, but nothing they say ever will.

Only seeing you again will do that.

Yours forever,

Clarisse

I sighed. Poor Clarisse. How her heart must have ached for Andre. I didn't even know her and still wanted to cry. The letter dropped to my lap.

Uncle Andre, why did you leave her?

A soft knock. "Wendy?"

Mom.

I stuffed the letter under my pillow again. "Come in."

She entered with quiet little steps as if I were a sick patient in the hospital.

I pulled my knees to my chest and wrapped my arms around them.

She sat on the bed and faced me, one leg hanging off the edge. "I felt terrible having to tell you about our decision. I—"

"Then why did you, Mom?" My voice was a sharp knife.

"It seemed like something a husband and wife should compromise on." Her voice remained calm.

I shook my head. "You and I never would've argued about this if it weren't for him. I would've asked you if I could go on a date. You would've said yes or no, and I would've accepted your answer."

"Aw, come on, it's not so bad." She slapped me playfully on the leg and left her hand resting there. "Summer will be here before you know it, you'll turn fifteen, and you'll be able to go out any weekend you like. Maybe twice."

"That's not so much the point as you and I having to start doing things his way. What if his idea of compromise means you giving in more to what he wants than he does to you? Doesn't that remind you of anything?"

She withdrew her hand. "We're not talking about your dad. Daniel is nothing like Pete was when we were married to each other." Worry lines appeared between her eyebrows, and she got that far-off look she used to get when she'd think about Dad.

She didn't deserve any bad memories worming their way into her mind.

I regretted causing that and softened my voice. "I know you want me to say I'm okay with this dating rule, but I can't. Not yet." I sighed and looked sideways at her. "Maybe never."

She stared at me.

"I think I need to be by myself right now. All right?"

She stood and walked to the door. She looked at me once more before turning the knob and leaving.

I had to get out of that house.

Chapter 11

I peeled off my clothes and searched my chest of drawers for sweatpants and a t-shirt. In a jiffy, I dressed, pulled on my most comfortable running shoes, and tucked a few bucks into one sock.

Without knowing or caring where I'd wind up, I sneaked out of the house and took off running. If anybody expected me to ask permission first, too bad. If Alice expected an invitation to join me, she could forget it. Nobody tells you the truth beforehand—that family life can be stifling. Being alone in the open spaces was what I needed.

On foot instead of in a car, I got an up-close introduction to the new neighborhood, down to the flowers planted next to mailboxes and pets relaxing on the front lawns. People on the sidewalk nodded or said hello, and little kids waved. Then I entered a commercial area filled with well-kept storefronts and smiling shoppers. The scents of potpourri and candles wafted from boutiques. Soon buildings with boarded-up or broken windows lined the street, with friendly smiles nonexistent. Garbage littered the sidewalks, stench rising to assault my nostrils. With my bravado fading, I veered off in the direction of the grocery store we frequented. I could use a bottle of water anyway.

I jogged in front of an animal clinic, closed for the day. That might be a good place to apply for a job once I got a driver's license. Visions of a veterinary career, with me the hero of dogs and owners alike, flowed in a daydream until I reached the side of a multi-story building. Painted on its brick wall: Villa Maria Retirement Residence. My shoes squeaked with the sudden stop.

I'd run farther than I realized, but maybe God meant for me to wind up here, the place I'd mentioned to Sam for Mrs. V. At that time, I'd seen it only from the front while riding in the car. I turned the corner, yanked open the glass door, and stepped inside.

"May I help you?"

Panting, I introduced myself to the wary middle-aged woman behind the front counter. An expensive-looking flower arrangement at the end dwarfed her head.

"Are you sure you're in the right place, dear?" She probably thought I needed a doctor.

"Yes. Just give me a minute please." I forced a deep inhale.

"Take your time."

I nodded and exhaled slowly. "I'd like some information for a friend of mine. An elderly lady with Alzheimer's."

She smiled. "Well, aren't you sweet." She removed a couple of pamphlets from a wall rack. "Here's a brochure about the residence in general." She handed me the first one. "And this one is about our senior services in particular."

I skimmed the color photographs on their covers. "Thanks."

"Your friend can receive assisted living or, if necessary, twenty-four-hour care. Here's a fee schedule. Does she have an adult family member to help her?"

I twisted my lips toward one cheek. "Yes. I'll give him this information."

If only he'd read it.

I raced back toward home, careful to avoid any streets marked with desolation. My pace slowed to a brisk walk as I reached my neighborhood. Every leg muscle ached. By the time my feet hit the cement of my front porch, I was beat.

Belle met me in the kitchen, but otherwise all was quiet inside. I poured a big glass of water and chugged it down. Her water bowl was dry, so I filled it.

"Need a snack, Belle?" I offered her a dog biscuit. She accepted it happily though not greedily. She must've had dinner already.

I grabbed a box of graham crackers along with the Villa Maria brochures, and we headed to my room.

Everyone's bedroom door was closed. I'd been wondering if I'd have time to myself in a stepfamily, but maybe I'd have more of it than I originally thought.

My phone sat on the dresser in my room where I'd forgotten it when I took off. That was stupid. What if I'd run into trouble, with no one knowing where I'd gone?

Ah, Sam had e-mailed me.

TRY TO COME BY TOMORROW.

Oh, I planned to. I responded: OK.

I'd look over the brochures and prepare my case to present to Tony. Maybe take them to school in the morning.

But first, letters to read. I reached under my bed for the envelopes and then perched on the edge of the mattress.

Dear Andre,

These past several months have felt like an eternity without you. If it weren't for your letters assuring me that your love is true, I would lose my mind.

My father has pressured me to go out with the son of a man he works with. Of course I don't want to, and I've made every excuse I can think of not to.

Mama understands better than Daddy that my feelings for you are not something I can turn off easily like a water faucet. But she is ill now with cancer and has no strength to argue with him, if she ever would.

In spite of your words of devotion, I sometimes worry that you'll fall in love with someone else without meaning to. It might simply happen with a pretty girl you meet in Kentucky. Or you might give in to your parents' pressure and marry

Anita.

I hope I don't sound like I'm whining. I don't like that in other people.

Please pray for my mama to get better, even though the doctor doesn't think she will.

Love,

Clarisse

How awful. Besides being separated from Andre and afraid of losing him to another girl, she was losing her mother. If her mother died, who would she have to confide in?

If I didn't have Mom to talk to … My stomach flipped. I'd always relied on her to listen to my troubles, and I needed her now more than ever. Should an argument over dating ruin our relationship? Clarisse's romance was much more serious than mine, but she hadn't let it spoil her love for her mother.

I folded the letter into its original shape and glided it into its envelope, careful not to tear the aging paper, as though Clarisse's heart lay in my hands.

The next envelope's postmark was illegible.

Dear Andre,

I've arrived safely home again. At least I have to call it home or risk my family's suspecting my secret. My real home will always be with you.

Don't worry. My cousin in Illinois will never reveal that

we were married there—

I squealed and bounced my butt on the mattress. Married! Clarisse and Andre got married!

—while I stayed with her. I have too much dirt on her she wouldn't want others to know, although I probably would never use it.

I'm so happy you and I had this past month together. It was the best, most glorious month of my life and will sustain me until I see you again. And hopefully, by that time, we will be able to be together always.

However, I have some sad news. My mother is not doing well, and the doctors don't expect her to live more than a few more weeks, a month at most. I'm thankful that God allowed me to return home in time to see her again and comfort her before she passes.

As I suspected would happen, my entrance into college must be postponed—

She was young, just out of high school! Maybe seventeen? Kids started school earlier back then.

I'll search for a job here to be near my family and help out with Mama's doctor bills.

With my family's lives centered around Mama now, there's no more talk of my dating anyone. For that, I'm grateful.

Your loving wife,

Clarisse

Clarisse had so much to handle on her own, and she was still a teenager. How could she cope? She needed Andre, so why couldn't they be together?

A door clicked open in the hall. Someone was moving about, perhaps Mom. I got up and peeked out. Alice spotted me, and without saying a word, entered the bathroom between her room and mine and slammed the door.

Chapter 12

I placed my bowl of cereal next to Alice's at the breakfast table and pulled out a chair. Only the two of us occupied the kitchen, ready for school. "I'm sorry about everything I said yesterday."

She rubbed her lips together between her teeth and released them with a smack. "I guess you were just trying to support your case for dating. Add 'lawyer' to your list of possible careers."

"I don't think so, but thanks for the compliment." If it was a compliment. "And for giving me another chance."

She got up from the table and walked out of the room before I realized she never said she accepted the apology.

David and I sat on the ground under the tree in front of school. He rested his forearms on his knees and turned his head sideways to look into my face. "What's wrong?"

I looped my arms under my jean-covered legs. "How can you tell?"

"You're so quiet. Usually you're all, you know, bubbly in the morning." He lifted his hands and rotated his palms in the air, his eyes big and wide.

I laughed. "I hope I'm not that obnoxious."

"No, but what's wrong?"

"My mom and I had an argument." I cut my eyes toward him. "About dating."

"Yeah?"

"Until I turn fifteen, I can go out only once every other week."

He shrugged. "So?"

His casual attitude grated my nerves. He should care, if anyone should. "What about us? Don't you want to go out any more?" The heat rushed to my face.

He placed a hand on my arm. "Sure I do. But I can't drive yet anyway. And Ben?" He blew a puff of air from between his lips. "Don't count on us getting invited to go out with him and Carla every week."

"Oh." I hadn't thought of that.

"Anyway, being restricted to going out every other weekend doesn't mean we can't get together for other occasions."

"What do you mean?"

"What if my parents have a barbeque or something, and I can invite someone?"

"True." My mind's eye pictured dinners at my house, Christmas parties, birthday parties.

"And I'll attend your track meets, and you can go to my baseball games. At least sometimes, when we can each get there."

"Yeah."

"So, problem solved?" He grinned.

"Solved." I kissed him on the cheek.

"Wow, our first PDA."

I giggled.

Steps toward achieving girlfriend status:
9. Public display of affection (Check.)

"Better watch out." He winked, but the look in his eye told me he didn't mind the risk of getting caught.

The bell rang, and he stood and pulled me to my feet.

"Wendy, come meet the guys." David intercepted me carrying my lunch tray and led me over to a noisy table full of jocks.

I glanced one table over where Alice sat with her back turned in my direction. Gayle chatted to Alice from across the table without noticing me. I'd only be a minute anyway, done before they missed me.

The muscular bodies at David's table parted. Someone pulled up an extra chair.

"Have a seat." David took the tray from my hands and set it down.

"Maybe for just a little while." I checked Alice and Gayle.

Gayle's dark-brown complexion reddened to a deep burgundy, her full lips set firmly together.

Alice must've taken notice of Gayle's face because she turned around. Within half a second, she scanned me, my tray, and the empty seat next to me. "Seriously?" she said loud enough for conversation in our corner of the cafeteria to grind to a halt. She glared, clenching her teeth.

David rolled his eyes and sat down, scowling at her.

"I'm sorry," I mouthed to Alice, my eyebrows tilted downward at the outsides.

"Whatever." Alice turned back around and continued eating.

No use in trying to go back to our table with Alice in that kind of mood. I stayed with the jocks.

On the bus ride home, I tried to explain to Alice what happened at lunch. "I wasn't planning to eat with them, just visit for a minute, but you got so mad I figured I may as well."

Her mouth open, she pressed her tongue against her teeth and rolled her eyes. "You know, it's not like you don't see him before school and between classes. All Gayle and I ask for is about fifteen minutes of your time at lunch. You even talk to him right after you finish eating, before lunch break is over."

I closed my eyes and hung my head. "I know, and I understand what you're saying." I raised my face to hers again. "He just wanted me to meet his friends, and I didn't want to tell him no. They're nice, by the way. Not at all what we thought about football and baseball jocks."

She shrugged. "I guess you'd rather be part of a more popular crowd."

I snorted. "Come on. You know me better than that."

"Well, just remember—less than six months ago, you were a nobody just like Gayle and me." With that, she picked up a book, opened it, and didn't look up until we reached our house.

All right, then.

With the Villa Maria brochures in my back pocket, I left Alice waiting for Adam after school and took off on my bike for Mrs. V's.

My hands trembled at the prospect of presenting Tony with the information I carried. I prayed for courage.

He wasn't there—again. Just as well. I'd have a chance to show them to Mrs. V and Sam first. I parked my bike alongside her front porch. Sam opened the door and let me in.

"Dad goes out every afternoon to run errands," he explained. He handed me a canned soft drink and then sat on the recliner.

"Thanks." I set the can on the coffee table.

Mrs. V already sat on the sofa but didn't speak.

I sat next to her and opened the general-information brochure. "Look what I picked up for you, Mrs. V."

She showed no interest in it, preferring to pick at a thread poking out of a seam on the sofa. That tore a little hole in my heart.

I reached out to hand the brochure to Sam. "This place is even nicer than it looks on the outside."

The front door opened. I pulled the brochure back and sat up straight.

Tony stopped still as a block of granite, his narrowed eyes zeroing in on the paper in my hands. "What's that?" His voice boomed.

Mrs. V jerked her head up with the startled face of a reprimanded infant.

Goosebumps ran along my arms, but I held my head high and spoke in a voice oozing confidence—something I didn't actually feel. "Mr. Villaturo, I happened to be near the Villa Maria Retirement Residence and asked for these brochures for Mrs. V."

His eyes widened to reveal red lines tracking through the whites.

I swallowed hard. "It's a very nice place."

The red spread to his entire head and neck, including his ears.

"They have special services for people who need help taking care of themselves."

He snorted like a bull through his fleshy nose.

"I even brought a price list." By the end of my speech, my voice weakened to a pitiful squeak.

"You've got a lot of nerve." He yanked the brochure from

my hand.

I jolted. "I was just trying to help."

"What makes you think I haven't looked into this already? I don't need your help to take care of my own mother."

I should have shut up right then and there, but I couldn't stop myself. "She's lived in Louisiana since forever. How can you think of taking her so far away?" I willed myself not to cry.

But the sound of crying filled the air just the same.

Tears rolled down Mrs. V's cheeks, her shoulders keeping rhythm with her sobs. She looked at Tony and me like a fearful child whose parents were fighting.

My hand went to my mouth. "I'm sorry, Mrs. V. I'm so sorry."

With Sam's face in my peripheral vision, I stood up. It was impossible to know how much he'd understood of my conversation with Tony.

I squeaked out my final plea. "I love her, and I want her to stay." Good sense told me to edge toward the door.

"I'd appreciate your staying out of our business. If you weren't a friend of Sam's…"

Their business? I was the only one who'd spent any time with her the last few years—not them. I was the one who discovered something was wrong with her. If only she could say those things herself. "I think I love her more than you do!" I yelled at Tony. I'd thought it all along, and it slipped right out of my mouth.

Tony's voice growled. "Young lady, you don't know me or anything about my relationship with my mother." His hands balled into fists. "I think you'd better leave. Now."

I tore out of the house with the sound of Sam's footsteps behind me.

At the bottom of the porch, he grabbed my arm and spun me around. "My father is not a monster!" Sam's nasal voice roared, shaking me to my bones. I never wanted to hear or see him that angry again.

I yanked my arm free and raced toward my bike. I never wanted to see him again at all.

"Stop!" He chased me as I clumsily mounted the bike and tried to take off, my feet slipping from the pedals.

I finally gave up and rested on the bike seat with my legs spread on either side. My head hanging, I let the tears flow at last. Mrs. V was going to be taken, and there was nothing I could do to stop it. Not since Mom and Dad's divorce had I felt so helpless, unable to hang onto someone I loved.

Sam wrapped his arms around me, and I let him. He held me loosely for a minute. I inhaled a deep, shaky breath.

"Okay?" He lifted my face with one finger and looked into my eyes.

"It hurts so bad." I wiped my cheeks with the heel of my hand.

"I know." His voice was low and deep as he rubbed my

back.

At the street, a car had stopped, its motor running. Its occupant on the passenger side stared at us.

I gasped. David.

Our eyes met for a second, and then his brother's car sped away.

I phoned David as soon as I got to my room.

Please, God, let him answer.

Just when I thought the call would go to his voice mail, he picked up.

"Hi," I whispered.

Dead air space.

"David, I don't know what you thought you saw, but—"

"I saw you with some guy." His voice held an edge of hurt.

"Sam's just a friend."

"Sam." He mocked.

"He's Mrs. V's grandson. That's all."

"Looked like more to me."

"I'd just had an argument with his father."

"So you're friends with the whole family."

"No matter what I say, you're going to read the wrong thing into it, aren't you." I said it as a fact.

He took an audible breath. "You know what kills me— other than the fact that you've never mentioned him before, even once—is that I made the effort to try to see you. I called your number but it went to voice mail so I called your house and asked your mother if I could stop by, since Ben was going to drive close to your neighborhood. She told me you'd gone to Mrs. V's and I could run by there."

"I really appreciate that."

"Do you? You'd just told me today that we could only go out together every other weekend. Was that the truth, or did you want to reserve some weekends for Sam?"

"You're calling me a liar? I can't *even*." I ended the call.

Pressing my hands to the sides of my head, I propelled myself backward onto the bed. What was wrong with everybody?

I tried to be nice, to be a good girlfriend for David, a good sister to Alice, a good daughter for Mom and Papa D, and to look out for Mrs. V. It seemed everyone had something against me for no good reason. They judged me without taking the time to listen or even to get to know me at all, like Tony.

I sighed and executed a roll-over-stomach-slide off the bed. I'd rather think about Clarisse's problems. Anything to get my mind off this mess. I reached under the bed and pulled out the envelopes.

Where was the next one? Here.

Dear Andre,

I'm touched that you tried once again to communicate to your parents about me, but I'm not surprised that they refused to listen or see a remote possibility of us having a future together. I think it was a good idea you had, to mail that letter from another part of Kentucky so they wouldn't know exactly where you are.

Part of what both sets of parents say is true—marriage is hard enough when two people come from similar backgrounds, which we certainly don't. A man and a woman are asking for trouble when they're not the same color—

Not the same color? Like black and white? That would explain a lot.

—and there's always someone who'd like to stick their nose into someone else's business and make an issue of it. But at any rate, with the way your parents feel, and mine too, it's best for none of them to know anything about our marriage until we can live together far from Bayou Calmon. Maybe after that, or after others like us become more commonplace, we'll gain acceptance.

It's too soon right now for me to leave, with my mama's recent passing. The whole family is so sad without her, and I want to be with my daddy and brother and sister for a little while to make sure they'll be okay. I know you need to stay in Kentucky a while longer to make money if we're to have a comfortable life together somewhere that mixed marriages are legal, so I can accept us being apart right now if you can.

We should be careful to hide the fact that we're married from everyone we meet and not let on, even with people we think we can trust with that information. Please don't tell anyone you work with. You never know when someone up there has family or friends down here. After all, I have a cousin up north.

Until we are together again ...

All my love,

Clarisse

Clarisse sounded like such a sweet girl, kind and considerate. All she wanted was to live her own life.

Was that asking so much?

Chapter 13

The next morning on the bus, Alice treated me like a stranger, civil but distant. I told myself she couldn't keep up her little performance indefinitely. Plus there was no longer a reason for her to.

No David waited for me on the front lawn.

A whimper escaped my throat. I stiffened my back and put on a poker face, determined not to let anyone guess that my once happy world had shrunk into a hard, lifeless rock.

It wasn't my imagination that all eyes glued on me as I walked into the cafeteria at lunchtime, but not like when everyone first learned David and I were a couple. David surely had told his friends what he *thought* he'd caught me doing with Sam, and it didn't take long for that kind of thing to get around the entire freshman class.

Carrying my tray, I passed the jock table with no intention of stopping. David and the jocks hunkered over their lunch all of a sudden, intensely interested in chowing down. No one looked up.

With a deep breath and my head high, I approached my usual table. Alice and Gayle were missing. I scanned the room and spotted them at the brainiacs' table. No place had been left open for me.

Nowhere did anyone try to catch my eye or motion me to join them. Like a virus, the shunning had spread.

My last hope was Jennifer's table, but it had filled. She chattered with the other ballerinas, apparently unaware of my nomad status.

At last I located a table being vacated, with only a couple of people remaining at one end. I sat down facing the windows that covered an entire wall. With little appetite, I took a bite of baked potato. It stuck somewhere inside my tightened chest. I raised my head and tried to force it down.

The hollow-eyed girl in the glass stared back at me, her mouth twisted. She was miserable and alone.

I bit my lip. If only Sam were there. He'd make me feel better.

He understood and appreciated me, in spite of having known me for less than two weeks. Even hearing-impaired, he was more like me than anyone else I'd ever met. Animal lover. Artist. And we'd both been challenged in communicating with others for most of our lives.

But Sam wasn't a part of my everyday world and never would be. He had to go back to his own world very soon. And he'd take one of the best parts of this one—Mrs. V—with him when he left.

I had to get out of there before I screamed. I grabbed my purse, and leaving my tray on the table, ran from the cafeteria.

Outside, I phoned Mom, my vision blurred and nose runny. Through my sobs, I begged her to come get me, and she agreed without asking why. At least I could still count on her.

I slumped down into the grass with my back against the cafeteria's brick wall and pretended to check my phone messages. Even though there wouldn't be any. But at least I didn't have to face anyone.

A car horn tapped out three beats. I got up and stepped around the building to see the street.

Mom.

"Do you want to tell me what happened?" She squinted as I strapped into my seatbelt.

"Let's just say that dating David is no longer an issue. We had an argument last night about my being friends with Sam."

She sighed. "I'm sorry, honey. You know I never wanted anything like that to happen."

"And Alice …" I shook my head. "We were better off as casual friends than sister-friend hybrids."

"Now that's something we can work on together. Stepfamilies usually have difficulties adjusting in the beginning."

"I hope you're right."

"What's her beef?" She eased the car into traffic.

"Mostly David. So she'll be happier now."

"Still, we need to sit down as a family and talk to work

this out. She should understand that you may not always share the same friends."

"Mom!" I slapped my hand over my mouth.

She jerked the steering wheel, her eyes huge. "What is it?"

"I forgot to sign out!"

"Hooo." She held a hand to her chest. "Okay, I'll call the office and say you felt so sick we both forgot. There are different kinds of sick, and sick at heart is the worst kind."

I took a deep breath and exhaled. "Thanks, Mom."

"Look at you, breaking a rule for a change." She chuckled.

I'd broken a lot more than that.

After a family dinner where only Adam and his dad had anything to say, I begged off cleanup duty and took Belle to my room.

The past two days had finally caught up with me, and I could've easily gone right to sleep. But there were letters left to read.

Dear Andre,

I love you so much, and I get so tired of living this lie. I want to use your name and declare to the world that I'm your wife. The feeling was strongest when I applied for and then started my new job. All those forms to fill out. And all the other girls asking me if I was married or had a boyfriend. I guess it's easier for a man because you don't change your name when you get married. You're always the same person no matter what.

Around people in Bayou Calmon, I sometimes forget to use Freeman when I sign my name—

Wait. Freeman? As in Gayle Freeman? I shook my head. That must be a fairly common name.

—for any reason, and instead begin to write Broussard. I catch myself as soon as I write the B, and luckily my middle name is Belinda, so no one suspects a thing.

In spite of everything, that little coincidence makes me smile. I hope it makes you smile too.

Love always and forever,

Clarisse

She tried so hard to keep her spirits up, and she couldn't even be her real self.

I understood how she felt.

With the letter in my hand, I nodded off and dreamed of Andre and Clarisse living in a little gray shack in Bayou Calmon.

They started arguing and then transformed into David and me.

I awoke close to midnight and changed into my pajamas. My phone lay on the dresser, connected to its charger. I pulled out the cord.

Sam and I hadn't communicated since the fateful previous afternoon. And we needed to.

IT'S LATE, BUT I WOKE UP AND THOUGHT I'D E-MAIL YOU.

A reply came immediately. He was up too.

I'M GLAD YOU DID. I NEED TO TALK TO YOU. IN PERSON. CAN YOU COME BY? THE SOONER THE BETTER.

I'LL TRY TOMORROW.

It was time to exchange phone numbers so we could text. But I'd rather hear his voice.

Chapter 14

Someone who's experienced an embarrassing moment at school like I had the day before doesn't look forward to going back. But I'd had so many such moments in my life, I'd learned to bear the pointing and the stares and act like I couldn't care less. Some were probably in my imagination anyway.

But just in case, I got off the bus and focused straight ahead without looking anyone in the eye.

David sprung into my line of vision. I slowed my forward movement to what must've looked like a prowl. He couldn't be walking right toward me, could he?

He was.

My battered heart jerked to life.

"Hey." He didn't smile, but speaking even one word was a good sign.

"Hi, David." I stopped, keeping my distance at a few feet. He was like an approaching squirrel I didn't want to frighten away.

"I was wondering if we could talk in private at your house after school. Ben can drop me off."

My heart sprouted wings. "I guess that can be arranged."

Surely Mom would allow it. But Sam—well, I'd have to postpone him for one day.

"Okay. I'll text you when I'm on my way." Still no smile.

"Sure." I stayed put as he turned around and walked toward the main building.

Did this mean we still had a chance?

Shockers. Alice and Gayle actually kidded around with me at our lockers before class, though they made no mention of David. Then they both migrated back to our regular table for lunch. They looked up when I sat down next to Alice.

Gayle smiled, her eyes not as sparkly as usual, more like she pitied me. But I'd take what I could get.

The three of us ate in silence for a couple of minutes. Apparently it was up to me to start a conversation. "I've been reading some letters written to my great-uncle."

Alice whipped her head toward me. "To Andre? How'd you get those?"

"Mattie gave them to me as we were leaving Bayou Calmon."

"Funny you never said anything." She jabbed a piece of chicken with her fork.

I ignored her and spoke directly to Gayle. "My Great-uncle Andre Broussard was my Grand-mere Robichaud's older brother. He left Louisiana because of a girl he fell in love with, and nobody in the family wants to talk about him."

She raised her eyebrows. "Interesting."

"Yeah. What I've learned so far from the letters this girl wrote to him is that neither of their families wanted them to get married, but—"

"Why not?" Alice fired the question at me.

"It was the early 1960s." I hesitated. "They weren't the same color, so both families knew the odds were stacked against them for a marriage to survive."

"You mean—" Alice started.

Gayle shoved her words at us. "Maybe she was Creole."

Alice frowned. "What's that?"

"People who've been in Louisiana since it was first settled. They're a mixture of black, French, Spanish, and sometimes Native American. There's some Creole in my family, not just African-American."

"The letters don't mention race, only her last name, her maiden name." A little voice told me not to say it, but I argued back that it had to be a common name. "It's Freeman."

Gayle picked at a nail cuticle. "That's a very common name."

"I figured you'd know."

"So is Broussard."

I blinked. True, it was, but what an odd thing to say.

Gayle took a sip of water. "Let's talk about something else."

But we didn't. We didn't talk about anything else at all.

"Good luck with David." Mom hugged me. "If it's meant to work out, it will."

I knew one thing—I was tired of trying to fit someone else's idea of who I should be or how I should act.

A worst-case scenario of David and me arguing about Sam played in my head, followed by one of David asking me for forgiveness and us making up and kissing.

Ben's car pulled into the driveway. "That's him now. I'll go meet him, and we can talk outside."

"Okay. I'll keep Adam close to me so he'll let you alone."

The door closed behind me as Mom shouted, "Adam!" and Ben backed down the driveway.

"Hey." David's green eyes squinted in the sunlight. They matched his t-shirt. He'd washed his face, his hairline still damp. He smelled of soap, something herbal.

My willpower slipped. I wanted to lean against him. "Let's go to the backyard."

We sat on the edge of the deck and rested our feet in the grass, still green before the first frost.

"I've been thinking a lot about you and me."

I held my breath.

He focused on a distant point in the yard. "I'm not some kind of control freak, but I don't like your being friends with other guys. At least not *that* kind of friend, the kind you are with *him*." He picked up a small twig and began breaking pieces from it and tossing them into the grass.

Was he kidding? I rattled my head at the absurdity.

"Sounds like control freak to me. And exactly what do you mean by *that kind of friend*?"

He scowled. "You don't even see the problem."

The back door opened and Belle bounded into the yard. She ran straight up to David.

He pushed her away. "Get! Get off me."

I couldn't believe it! I grabbed Belle by the collar, though she'd barely touched him. "She's only trying to say hello. She obviously likes you." I'd never doubted her judgment of character before.

"I'm just not used to dogs and would rather not be around them. We've never had one at my house." He stood up and brushed himself off.

She hadn't gotten him dirty at all.

I stood too, ready to get back to the real issue. "I *don't* see a problem with my being friends with Sam."

"So you won't even try to understand my side? I thought you'd have some kind of explanation at least, and we could work things out."

"I already told you—I'd just had an argument with Sam's father. Mrs. V has Alzheimer's, and he wants to take her to Alaska."

"What difference does that make? You're not related to her."

My mouth gaped open, and I glared at him. "Now who doesn't understand? She's been like a grandmother to me."

"I still don't see what any of this has to do with us. But maybe you and I aren't ready to be … what's the word … exclusive."

"What are you saying?"

"I don't think we can be a couple as long as Sam's in the picture."

"Well, I don't think we can be a couple anyway. You can't accept the real me—or my dog."

He pressed his lips together in a thin line and stalked off, through the gate to the front yard.

I collapsed to my knees on the deck and buried my face in Belle's shoulder.

In a few minutes, the back door opened quietly and Mom came out. "He's gone."

She followed me to my room, and I crawled into bed. She covered me and then sat next to me on top of the covers.

"Would you play with my hair?" I whispered with my eyes closed.

"Sure, sweetie."

She gently twirled sections of hair between her fingers, and I drifted off to sleep.

I awoke with my last words to David in my head. *The real me.*

Who was I, anyway?

Just when I thought I'd figured it out, felt comfortable in my own skin, and people started liking me, some of those same people rejected me.

Was I selfish? A bad sister? No, but Alice thought so.

I was a super-caring person, wasn't I? But I'd hurt Mrs. V, and I hated myself for doing that. So was I simply a meddler like Tony said?

After all this time, maybe I still didn't know how to be a true friend.

And had David seen something regarding my feelings for Sam that I didn't recognize myself?

I sat up.

Sam.

I rubbed my tight neck muscles. Because of David, I'd missed the chance to see him and Mrs. V, but Sam was one too many things to think about for the moment. I got out of bed.

In the bathroom, I splashed water on my face and brushed my teeth. One letter remained to read before starting my homework.

Dear Andre,

I hope you'll be happy to learn that we're going to have a baby—

What? I pinched my lower lip.

—but I'm so afraid. I won't be able to hide the fact for long. What will I tell people? How will I explain to my family?

What will she do?

Please, please come home, and let's tell our families the truth about our marriage. If you won't agree to that, please at least come and get me. I can meet you somewhere in the middle of the night, and we can drive far from Bayou Calmon before anyone realizes I'm missing.

I can't have this baby and raise it without you. I just can't! Our future depends on you.

If you love me, come soon. I pray to God for you to be here soon.

Love,

Clarisse

I was afraid for the future, too.

Chapter 15

After a restless night, I e-mailed Sam before breakfast.

SORRY I DIDN'T COME BY YESTERDAY. TODAY FOR SURE. OK?

OK. DON'T FORGET. IT'S IMPORTANT.

WANT TO SWAP PHONE NUMBERS LATER SO WE CAN TEXT?

GOOD IDEA.

Sam didn't explain the urgency, but my gut told me that time was running out for Mrs. V, and I needed to see her before it was too late. If Tony stayed true to his daily routine, he wouldn't be there, at least not when I arrived.

I only needed to get through the day at school. Only.

It's incredible how, when you're dying to run into someone you like at school, you rarely do. When you break up with that person, he's everywhere.

David and I had only two classes together, but he haunted me in the halls outside every class like the ghost of Christmas past. He even showed up at the same time I dropped off a form at the athletic office. Again when I ran an errand to the teachers' lounge. And sat in the row behind me at an unscheduled assembly.

Fate stinks.

The pain of seeing David was like a toothache—constant, miserable, and with no hope of relief. And with all that exposure, I had to make sure I looked my best on the outside at all times, when my insides lay in shreds.

Fortunately, I was no longer the freshman topic *du jour*. Another girl had been caught smoking behind the gym with the assistant basketball coach.

If I'd known seeing Sam's face again would make me forget David's for a while, I would've been there sooner.

A drizzly Louisiana rain, the kind that makes you feel sticky instead of refreshed on a warm day, had dampened my hair and shoulders by the time I reached Mrs. V's.

Sam met me on the porch with a bath towel, grinning.

I grinned back, accepting the towel, and stroked it over my head. "Thanks. Now you see what I look like with frizzy hair."

"I think I like it." He crossed his arms over his chest, leaned back against the wall, and squinted his hawk eye. "It looks untamed, the way the Alaskan wilderness girls like to wear it."

"For that, you get this." I snapped him with the towel, and we both laughed.

He grabbed my arms, and for a second …

Then his smile collapsed. He loosened his hands and ran

them down the length of my arms, stopping at my hands and holding onto them.

His voice lowered. "We're taking Grandma next week."

Blood pounded between my ears, and I struggled against his grip. Like a defeated puppy, I sounded a tiny whimper.

"It's the best thing to do. Really, Wendy. She'll be in a place close to my dad's job, so he can check on her every day."

"But it's so soon." I drooped.

He let go of me slowly, as if I were a delicate crystal vase in danger of toppling over.

I squeezed my eyes shut and opened them again. "I'd like to go in and see her now."

He reached for the door handle. "Just prepare yourself. From day to day, even hour to hour, we never know what to expect."

With timid steps, I entered the house.

He held me back with a hand on my upper arm before I got very far. "You know I've never heard your voice, but the doctor said not to talk to her as if she's a child. Alzheimer's patients don't like that. It belittles them and can make them angry."

"Okay." Good thing he told me.

He let me go, and I moved farther into the living room.

She sat in Gus's recliner, almost swallowed by it, feet dangling above the floor. She wore a sweater with a hole in it.

She used to care about how she dressed.

"She likes sitting there most of the time." Sam positioned himself on the sofa where he would be able to read our lips.

"Hi, Mrs. V." I pulled up a kitchen chair and angled it next to her so we could see each other's faces.

"Hello." She smiled and patted my hand. "I'm going to go see my granddaughter soon." Then she spoke to Sam. "What's her name again?"

"It's Sarah, Grandma."

She turned back to me. "That's right—Sarah." She scratched a spot on the back of one of her hands. It blossomed red.

I touched her skin, as dry and thin as paper, and then looked at Sam. "Do you have any hand lotion?"

"There's some in her bathroom." He got up and brought it back in a couple of seconds.

"Alaska is supposed to be beautiful." I gently massaged lotion on her arms and hands, working it into her fingers. "It'll be nice for you to be there with Sarah and Sam."

She returned my smile.

"Look this way." Sam held his phone up, ready to take our photograph.

Tears blurred my vision, but I pasted on a smile. He captured the shot.

With confusion in her eyes, Mrs. V pulled her hands away from mine.

"Okay, I see you've had enough. Did you like getting

lotion rubbed on your skin?"

She stared at me as though seeing me for the first time.

"Thank you for letting me visit with you." My body trembled as I handed the lotion back to Sam. "I think I should go."

He set the bottle on the coffee table.

"Good-bye, Mrs. V." I leaned over and kissed her forehead.

Sam followed me out the door. He caught me by the shoulder and turned me to face him before I could escape the porch. He didn't make a sound. His silence told me he understood my hurt.

He wrapped his arms loosely around me, and I rested my head against his chest.

"I'll miss her so much. I don't know what I'll do without her. But it seems like she's gone already."

He couldn't have heard me, but he tightened his hold.

After a few seconds, I pushed to free myself, resisting the gravitational pull of his golden sun-eyes.

He touched the side of my face and pressed a slip of paper into my hand.

I nodded, got on my bike, and rode home.

"Mrs. V has to go live in Alaska."

Everyone at the dinner table stopped chewing and turned their attention to me.

"I tried to stop her son from taking her." The idea sounded ridiculous once I voiced it. Why had I thought I could succeed? I focused on my plate, my lips twisted.

Mom gently set down her fork. "I'm sorry, honey. I guess it was the only practical solution."

I blinked a few times and raised my eyes.

Papa D pressed his lips together before speaking. "I'm sorry too, Wendy. This is a tough thing for you to deal with." He sighed. "When are they leaving?"

"Next week. If Sam said which day, I don't remember."

"It must be extra hard that it's happening so quickly. Would you like me to go with you to visit her?" Mom reached across the table for my hand. I stretched out to meet hers.

"That's sweet, Mom, but I don't know. Let me think about it."

"Sure."

I searched Alice's face for a sign of sympathy. She'd lost her mother and surely understood my pain. But whatever Alice thought or felt, she kept it to herself.

The slip of paper Sam had given me contained his phone number. Before crawling under my covers for the night, I saved the number to my phone and began a text.

THANKS FOR EVERYTHING. LET ME KNOW WHEN YOU'RE PLANNING TO LEAVE. IF POSSIBLE, I'D LIKE TO SEE MRS. V ONE MORE TIME TO SAY MY FINAL GOOD-BYE TO HER.

And to you, Sam.

Holding the phone, I rested my hand in my lap and leaned against the headboard. Mrs. V and Sam's exit would leave an empty pit with no one in sight to fill it. And this was the end, an end like no other. No one would say, "We'll be out your way next summer," or "See you when our teams play each other again in the fall."

Sam must've thought of that before I did. That's why he stopped at only a hug. Or did he not feel anything special between us? That was hard to believe.

Either way, Mrs. V had given me the wonderful gift of a friend in Sam, and she didn't even know it.

Or did she?

Maybe she'd planned it all along, our meeting and becoming friends, knowing what we'd each find in the other. Weren't we two of her favorite people?

The phone double-pinged in my hand, and I startled. Sam had responded.

My breath caught. The image on the screen was beautiful, the most beautiful I'd ever seen.

Our heads close together, Mrs. V and I smiled in fluid lines of charcoal on white.

Grandmother and granddaughter.

Forever.

Chapter 16

The last place I wanted to be was a football game. No one should have to attend a sporting event feeling as sad as I did.

Just the same, Gayle's mom picked Alice and me up early Friday evening.

"It'll be fun to go to the game together," Gayle said for the tenth time.

Alice crossed her arms. "You can't mope about David every night."

She was either dispensing tough love or didn't care at all about my feelings. It was the first time she'd mentioned David's name since he and I officially called it quits. And it stung like a hypodermic needle.

But if that was a needle, losing Mrs. V and Sam would be a hammer to the belly.

Once I dragged myself into the stadium, the football spirit *was* catching, and the first cool night of the season energized me like I hadn't been in a while. Plus I'd worn a new sweater that happened to be in our school colors, royal blue and white. I'd make the best of the situation.

We climbed high into the bleachers because Alice and Gayle wanted to. "To watch the band formations," Alice said, although she had no desire to play her clarinet in the band. "Easier to see the plays from a distance," Gayle said. Alice and Gayle were much more into the whole football game experience than I was. All I really cared about was track and base—ugh, I refused to think about David.

Other freshmen filled our section below. Tookie spotted us and waved. We smiled and waved back. If she had gotten into track like us, we probably would've had a fourth member in our little group.

Kickoff. We jumped to our feet. We imitated the mascot and roared like lions, pawing the air along with the rest of the crowd. We settled back onto our seats, coughing from the vocal exertion and then laughing. If we continued like that until the end of the game, our throats would be raw.

The bodies in front of us lowered a few at a time as everyone else sat down too. Except one.

David.

How had I missed him?

He bent over someone.

I weaved my head to see better through the spaces.

Tookie!

My hairline pinched.

He spoke close to her ear. Her smile, the flush in her cheeks, the way she tossed her shiny auburn hair back with a flip of her head—she still liked him. Or a lot more.

They talked a minute longer. Then she scooted over, and

he sat next to her.

My fist pressed against the snake coiled around my insides.

Working a paint roller on Alice's bedroom walls Saturday morning got some of my anger and hurt over David out. Some of it.

I gritted my teeth and stretched, pushing and pulling the roller until I was a sweaty, paint-spattered mess.

With each stroke of the color—bright turquoise, but I didn't comment—Alice smiled bigger. Finally, I'd made up for abandoning her and Adam to go out with David while our parents were on their honeymoon.

"I'll help you paint your room too." She used a brush to trim along the molding and baseboards before I followed with the roller. "Any color you want."

I paused and tilted my head, puzzled and amazed by this girl who'd become my sister. "Okay, great."

I set the roller in the tray to soak up more paint. So *this* was the kind of thing families did for one another.

Chapter 17

On Sunday, Mom and I attended our old church for the last time, just the two of us. Her idea, not mine.

I wore my best skirt, a fitted pullover top, and a pair of dressy flats. Dressed to impress in case I ran into David. I dreaded seeing him, although I'd agreed to try to meet his parents again. But that was *before*. Going to a new church starting next week would be a good thing to help me get over him.

His family didn't show, or didn't sit where I could see them anyway. What a relief.

When Mass ended, Mom and I exited through the main doors. First step out, and I wanted to run back inside.

David stood at the foot of the steps with Tookie.

I stopped, and a little boy crashed into my Achilles tendon with hard oxfords. My teeth clenched and my eyes scrunched up. Tookie walked away and David looked up, right at me.

Not the expression on my face I wanted him to see. I smoothed my features and continued walking down the steps.

He blushed to the roots of his hair, like I'd caught him stealing from the collection basket. "Tookie's really very nice. She's changed a lot since last year."

"Yeah, I think I know her better than you do." I shoved past, almost flattening the music minister, and left David stunned. Or so I hoped.

Problem was, Tookie *was* very nice. And the kind of girl he'd like.

The possibility that *I wasn't* the kind of girl David liked invaded my thoughts like a wild blackberry vine, twisting and poking into the empty spaces. With thorns.

I carried a box of tissues into the backyard, sat under a tree, and bawled like a baby. Belle lay next to me, the focus of her brown eyes bouncing from one place to another like they did when she was worried.

The back door opened slowly.

Great. Daniel.

I turned my head toward the back fence. Maybe he'd go away.

"Wendy."

I blew my nose and faced him.

"Your mom told me what's been happening with David."

My mouth gaped open and then slammed shut, air rushing out my nose like a snorting bull's. She'd crossed the line. I tried to push myself off the ground, ready to go back into the house and have it out with her, but he held my shoulder.

"Wait. Before you get mad at her—she did it because she loves you. She asked me to give you my perspective of the situation."

I swallowed the ugly words working their way up my throat and collapsed on my butt again.

"May I?" He squatted a couple of feet from me without waiting for an answer.

"Just tell me quick what you have to say, please." I pursed my lips.

His expression was soft, his eyes compassionate. "I'm so sorry you got hurt." He paused and shook his head. "The reason I didn't want you or Alice to date yet is because I hoped you'd use this first year of high school to get to know more than one boy. Then you could decide whether it was worth spending a lot of time with only one."

I stared at him and struggled to keep from tearing up. *God, I don't need a lecture right now.*

"When you date someone exclusively before you've spent enough time together, and then you find out you're not cut out for each other, somebody gets hurt. I wanted to spare both of you girls that if I could."

I frowned. "It could happen anyway, anywhere down the line."

"True. But it hurts more when it's the first one you've ever loved and the only one you really know."

All I recognized was the hurt. But was it love?

His blue eyes reached into my soul. Maybe something similar had happened to him. For a second he morphed into the teenage boy he must've been a long time ago. Innocent, trusting, vulnerable.

He reached over and double-patted my knee. "And I want you to know that you can come to me as well as to your Mom with guy problems." He chuckled. "I'll be happy to share my limited knowledge about relationships."

I couldn't help but smile. "Thanks ... Papa D."

The last envelope wasn't opened. How'd I miss that? The fold at the top had worn and split in a couple of places, that's all. I finished the job with a small pair of scissors.

Dear Andre,

I'm so worried. I didn't receive a reply to my last letter. Why haven't I heard from you? Please tell me what's wrong. My heart is breaking.

Don't you care for me anymore? Are you seeing someone else?

My heart ached with the same questions about David. I sniffed and grabbed a tissue.

Maybe you're afraid to tell me that you don't want the responsibility of a baby. But I'd rather know the truth.

I lost my job when my belly grew too big to hide. My father and the rest of my family believed me when I told them the baby is yours but not that you married me before it was conceived in Illinois. I have no proof of our marriage at all, not even a wedding ring.

Desperate to hear from you,

Clarisse

I clutched the hem of my pajama shirt in my fist. Was that how it ended for Clarisse? Having a baby without its father? Not knowing what killed his love for her? How horrible!

But Andre couldn't have abandoned her. His family—my family—was the same one that produced Grand-mere, sweet Mattie, and Jerome.

If this was the final letter Clarisse had mailed to Andre and the last one he received, why didn't he open it? And how did the letters wind up in Mattie's tool shed?

I paced the room, rubbing my temple.

If I asked Aunt Renee about the letters, Mattie could get into trouble for taking them. There was nowhere else to go but the Internet.

I chose to sit at my computer for the benefit of a big screen and typed Andre Broussard into the search window.

A surprisingly large number of instances populated the screen, so I added the word Kentucky to my search.

With a slow scroll, I scanned for anything that might relate to Clarisse's account of Andre's life.

Then I found "Andre Broussard," "Kentucky," and "miner" in the same result.

I held my breath.

The headline for an article from a monthly newspaper dated 1961 read, "Young miner dies from asphyxiation."

My stomach flipped. The yellowed article had been scanned or photographed and placed on a personal website, along with accounts of other small mining tragedies. Probably none of these had made big news anywhere.

Fingers covering my lips, I read the details as far as they were legible.

"I found him, Clarisse," I whispered. "He didn't stop loving you—at least not by choice."

Chapter 18

I did *not* want to go to school Monday and be forced to witness David and Tookie's budding little romance. I would've much preferred a case of the flu that was going around. And that was saying a lot, considering how I hated throwing up.

But an algebra test was scheduled for Tuesday, and my overall grade needed the B-12 shot a class review would provide. So I got out of bed and took a shower.

With no enthusiasm, I pulled myself together with spandex, a belt, and makeup thick enough to act as an adhesive. If only I could paint on a fake smile like the Joker.

On the bus, I curled up in a seat by the window and next to Alice.

"I got another one." She pulled a greeting card out of a purse half the size of a box of Kleenex.

How she fit everything she needed into that little thing was a mystery to me.

"Let me see." I held out my hand.

"Just the outside." She drew the card back. "Promise?"

"Promise." What Jerome had written on the inside was probably nothing a nun couldn't read to her Mother Superior.

"That makes two per week since I met him." She grinned

and squeezed her shoulders together.

"It's pretty, Alice. He has good taste." I smiled.

Poor kid. Wait until her heart got broken someday like mine had. I just hoped it wouldn't be Jerome who broke it.

I handed the card back to her, and she added it to the rubber-banded stack in the purse. I turned toward the window.

Who did I see first thing when the bus pulled onto school property?

David. Of course.

As if on cue, Tookie shot across the lawn toward him. Together they joined the jock group near the steps.

This was going to be a long day.

After school, Alice, Gayle, and I sprawled on the shag area rug in my room. Algebra books lay waiting near our bare feet.

Gayle leaned her back and head against the bottom of my mattress. "Ugh. I'd rather do anything right now than study for an algebra test."

Alice lay on her stomach, propped up on both elbows. "Me too, but we pinky swore we'd study together for anyone's weakest subject. And this is definitely the weakest subject for all of us."

Gayle raised her head. "I kno-o-o-w."

I sat with my legs spread out and palms in the shag fibers, playing with them between my fingers. "I could tell y'all what

I found out about my Great-uncle Andre," I said in a perky voice. Then I lowered the perkiness level a notch. "It's sad, though."

Gayle wrinkled her nose. "I retract my earlier statement."

"I wouldn't mind hearing about it, since I *do* know some of the family." Alice glared at me.

She had a point. I should've been more considerate and kept Alice up-to-date on my discoveries. After all, she'd been nice enough to go on my fact-finding mission to Bayou Calmon. Even though she didn't help like I expected.

"Oh, all right. Let's hear it." Gayle sat up straight.

I bent my knees and drew my legs to the side. "Well, I didn't get a chance to tell y'all last time that Andre and the girl—her name was Clarisse—did get married."

Gayle's eyes widened until the cocoa-bean brown of her eyes was surrounded by white.

"First Andre went to Kentucky to work in the coal mines and left Clarisse in Bayou Calmon. But later she visited her cousin in Illinois, and she secretly married Andre there. They still didn't tell their families afterward. She went home—her mother had cancer—and Andre kept working in Kentucky. Later, Clarisse found out she was pregnant."

Alice gasped. Gayle froze, as still as a statue.

"The worst part was that after she told him, she didn't receive any more letters. The last one she sent to Andre begs him to tell her why she hasn't heard from him. It wasn't opened until I opened it. "

"What a jerk!" Alice scowled and sat up.

Gayle turned that burgundy color.

"But he didn't abandon her. He was killed in a mining accident. Suffocated. I found an article about it online."

"Oh, no. How terrible." Alice hugged her knees. "Do you think Clarisse ever learned the truth?"

"I don't know, but the letters wound up at my Aunt Renee's. That's how my cousin Mattie found them. Maybe they were sent there with his other belongings if Aunt Renee was listed as his nearest living relative."

Gayle shook her head, her expression grim. "Unbelievable," she muttered under breath. She turned away from me and cleared her throat. "We'd better study now." She picked up her algebra book and opened it but didn't appear focused on the pages in front of her.

I reached for my own book, watching her face. What was her deal? It wasn't like Gayle to be impolite or moody when one of us had something we wanted to talk about.

And I remembered the last time I'd heard someone else say the name Broussard. Gayle's father's first name was Bruce, but her mother called him Broussard.

Chapter 19

The worst part about the algebra test was that David sat a few seats in front of me, one row over. I hated alphabetized seating.

The back of his head and the occasional glimpse of his profile distracted me for the full forty minutes. I'd be lucky to get a D, a C minus at best.

After class, Tookie ambushed him in the hall, all big eyes and whispers. David had said she'd changed, but it looked like some of the old Tookie was creeping back.

Just as David had appeared at every turn the day after our break-up, now so did Tookie. With David.

He must've been interested in her all along, or he would've asked her to get lost. How could I have been so stupid?

Someone shouted my name in the cafeteria. I swung around carrying my lunch tray and crashed right into David.

My salad and carton of milk slid off the tray as he hopped one step back to avoid a direct hit.

The shocked look on his face was so funny, if I hadn't been furious with him, I would've burst out laughing. Instead, cuss words fought to escape my lips.

Neither of us apologized. He squatted to the floor and helped me pick up pieces of lettuce. That was my chance to say what I'd held in for too long.

I spoke under my breath, hoping no one else heard. "I can't believe you had the nerve to criticize my friendship with Sam, and you didn't even take a breath before you hooked up with Tookie."

His face turned as red as the cherry tomato that rolled past his foot. "It's not like that at all. We're just friends."

"Save it, David." I tossed my ruined lunch in the trash and headed for the vending machines.

Gayle slipped a vending-machine granola bar into her purse and turned away without noticing me. Her overstuffed book bag hung on her back.

"Hey, where are you going?" I shouted.

She glanced behind her and stopped. "Hey." She shifted the book bag with a rotation of her shoulders. "With the stress over the algebra test, I forgot I had a doctor's appointment." She rolled her eyes. "My dad should be in the office to check me out."

"I'll walk with you."

"Great." She squinted at my face, still warm from the cafeteria incident. "Are you okay?"

"Yeah." I swatted the air. "Just ran into David. Literally.

And I didn't exactly behave like Miss Congeniality."

She grimaced. "It must be hard seeing him in class and then all over school with Tookie. I hope it gets easier soon."

She cared.

We reached the administration office, where Gayle's dad leaned against the counter. "Hello, girls." His friendly face beamed at us, his complexion a lighter brown than Gayle's.

"Hi, Mr. Freeman."

"Hi, Daddy."

He turned back toward the lady who approached him from the other side. "Broussard Freeman, to check out my daughter Gayle for a doctor's appointment."

Gayle's mouth opened and then snapped shut. She searched for a place to look other than at me. But she couldn't ignore that her father had said the name Broussard right in front of us.

My mind loaded one question after another, and my eyes sought Gayle's face for answers.

She sighed. "I guess I'd better call you later."

Chapter 20

My phone rang as soon as I walked into the house. Gayle had timed the call perfectly. No surprise, coming from her.

"Are you home?" Her voice was all business.

Please don't be in a bad mood. "Yeah."

"We're in the car. I'm coming over."

In ten minutes, her father dropped her off.

She strode through the front door, purpose in her step. "Sorry I've been acting weird lately."

At least she started with an apology. But her face was unreadable. "I assume you have a reason?" I closed the door behind her.

"I do, but it's a … private kind of story." She nodded sideways toward Adam sitting on the living room floor. "Can we go to your room?"

"Sure."

"Where's Alice?"

"She's here, somewhere. Probably talking on the phone to Jerome."

"Find her. I may as well tell both of you at the same time."

I rounded up Alice, explaining that Gayle had something important to tell us. We met her in my room.

Alice climbed onto the bed. I sat on my bench at the end of the bed, Gayle in my desk chair.

Alice and I stared at Gayle and waited.

"Before I start, could I see those letters?"

I pulled the envelopes out of my top desk drawer, handed them to her, and then returned to the bench.

She shuffled through them and examined the postmarks. "These dates would be about right." She opened the first letter, scraping her teeth over her lips like she did at the starting block before a race.

Alice and I riveted our attention to Gayle's face as she scanned each line of the pages.

She finished reading and then closed her eyes for a couple of seconds. She took a deep breath and read the letter again before folding and placing it back in its envelope. "This is definitely my great-grandmother."

"No! Are you kidding?" Alice bounced to her knees on the mattress.

I popped off the bench. "Wait—did you say *great-*grandmother?"

"Yeah. She was just a teenager when she fell in love with Andre. And it was 1960. Do the math."

She knew I hated math. "Forget the math. Why have you been acting so strange about this? Why didn't you just tell me what you suspected?"

Instead of answering, she shoved the stack into my hand.

"Where's the one that says they got married?"

"This one, I think." I drew it out.

She read it and then looked up, tears pooling in her eyes.

The only other time I'd seen her cry was when she talked about John. "What? What is it?" She was beginning to scare me.

"My great-great-grandfather—Clarisse's father—didn't believe that Andre had married Clarisse. They'd kept their relationship so secret that no one could back up her claim of being married. She couldn't locate a copy of the marriage license before the baby was born—or maybe she didn't try. I'd heard that she wasn't sure which county they were married in. Back in the early sixties, before computers, tracking down something like that could take a lot of phone calls or letters."

"How did you know that, I mean, about the marriage license? She doesn't mention anything about not having proof until her last letter."

"My father told me the story when I was twelve. Clarisse kept hoping and telling everyone that Andre would come back and prove they were married, or at least contact her. When it didn't happen, she gave the baby—my grandfather—the first name Broussard to honor Andre but used her maiden name Freeman for his last name." Gayle paused. "She died of an infection soon after my grandfather was born."

"Oh, no." I covered my mouth with both hands.

Alice scooted off the bed. "What a horrible ending." She

sprung to Gayle's side and rested a hand on her shoulder.

"Obviously, Clarisse died not knowing that Andre had been killed, but thinking he'd stopped loving her." An edge in her voice sharpened with each sentence. "His family didn't do her or my great-great-grandfather the courtesy of telling them what really happened. All this time, my family believed that Andre didn't marry her—and maybe never intended to."

My stomach churned. Gayle was one of my two best friends, and my family had wronged her family terribly. "This is awful." I crossed my arms tightly over my chest and hung my head before raising it and facing her again. "Did anyone in your family try to find proof after Clarisse died?"

Gayle shrugged and then shook her head slowly. "Maybe, maybe not. People get busy living their own lives. Soon the story was mostly forgotten, except for an occasional telling like when my father told me. I suppose he waited until he thought I was old enough to handle it."

If only Grand-mere or her parents—my great-grandparents—had done the right thing. Why didn't they? "I'm so sorry for the part my family played in what Clarisse went through and not telling her what happened to Andre."

"Thank you." She sniffed and massaged her arms. "I think what upsets my father the most is that my grandfather grew up living with embarrassment. The Freemans were a respected Creole family and devout members of their church."

My body went cold. That little boy grew up feeling that

something was wrong with him because his father wasn't there, and he didn't know why. I understood that feeling too well. "I wish you hadn't waited so long to talk to me."

"Well, when you first started talking about Andre, I thought … there might have been a lot of Andre Broussards in Louisiana at that time." She chuckled. "Kinda like the Cajun version of John Smith, you know? You mentioned Bayou Calmon specifically, so I tried to remember where my great-grandmother was from and couldn't. My grandfather moved to New Orleans as a young man, and that's where my daddy was born and grew up. I didn't want to ask him if Bayou Calmon was the town he'd talked about with me two years ago because I didn't want to remind him of the whole sad story. But you said neither of the two families wanted them to get married, so I started putting the pieces together. Then when you said Clarisse's name, I knew it couldn't be a coincidence."

Alice stroked Gayle's back. "I'm surprised you could keep this to yourself. Weren't you eaten up inside?"

"Not as bad as you might think. It all happened so far in the past. It doesn't change anything about my life. At least now I can tell my father the true ending of Clarisse's story." Gayle took a deep breath and looked at me. "I'd ask you for those letters to show to him, but I know they're not yours to give." Her eyes wide and earnest, she twisted a corkscrew lock of her hair.

I read the hope in her face, but she was right. The letters

didn't belong to me. I placed my hand on Gayle's other shoulder, opposite Alice. "Maybe you should read them all while you're here." I set the stack on the desk near her.

Gayle nodded and placed her hand over mine. "Can you believe I was angry at *you* for a while, though? First, for digging up this old hurt my family endured that everyone wants to forget. And second, for being a descendant of the people who caused Clarisse and my grandfather pain."

"It's okay. We're okay." I hugged her, and Alice overlapped our arms with hers.

"Like you had any control over anything that happened." She patted our tangle of arms with a hand that stuck out.

I didn't even have control over what happened in my own life. Like Clarisse, no matter how much I loved someone, I couldn't control whether they would have the ability to love me back. Or would want to. Or could stay.

Chapter 21

Because of the special relationships I had with Alice and Gayle, my thoughts eventually turned to those I had with David and Sam, spinning in circles while I prepared a batch of cookies from a roll of dough.

Gayle and I were able to get past a scandal that had caused both of our families confusion and misery, and we remained friends. Alice and I were able to understand how to live together and respect each other's individualism, and we became better sisters.

I plopped lumps of chocolate chip cookie dough onto a baking pan.

The three of us would always find ways to work things out, I was certain. No matter how tough a situation we found ourselves in, on opposite sides. We could disagree about all kinds of things but reach a compromise. We could forgive one another for petty offenses, knowing the offender would strive to do right next time. We didn't hold grudges. We supported one another.

So why were relationships with guys so *difficult*?

I shoved the pan into the oven and a leftover wad of dough into my mouth.

Sam had remained a friend while David had become a boyfriend. But I'd gotten to know Sam not long after I'd gotten to know David, and I liked them both. Just for different reasons. I'd already argued with and forgiven Sam a number of times. Yet forgiving David wasn't so easy. Was the difference that Sam and I were friends—and only friends?

My head pounded.

When David and I started dating, we stopped trying to see the other's point of view like friends. But why? Did dating automatically make him not my friend anymore? Why should one destroy the other?

I rubbed my temples and searched the kitchen cabinet for aspirin. Found it.

If I'd started dating Sam first, I was pretty sure I'd still be able to talk things out with him when we disagreed. Shouldn't I be able to do the same with David?

Maybe it was possible for David and me to start from the beginning and learn to like each other again. Or maybe it wasn't.

I stuffed myself with cookies all evening.

Chapter 22

The next day, I decided to do my best to behave like I had before David and I went out on our first date. Actually, the way I acted way before that. When we were only casual friends and nothing more.

Basically, I would conduct myself like Nothing. Bad. Ever. Happened.

When Alice and I arrived at school, she headed to the music room, and I made a spot for myself on the ground under the tree. David didn't own that tree. But if he showed up, that would be okay. Maybe even serendipitous.

The crowd of jocks collected near the steps, gathering mass by the minute. David was probably in there somewhere.

Soon Tookie got dropped off by her mom and came along, passing near the tree.

"Hi, Tookie." I gave her my best smile.

She slowed down. "Hi, Wendy. What's up?"

"Nothing." I hadn't planned before speaking to her, and I grappled for a topic. "Have you joined any clubs?" Good one. "I signed up for the art club."

She lowered herself to the ground and sat next to me. "No, I couldn't decide on one. But I'm pretty sure I'll try out for the flag team for next year. I've sort of gotten into football."

Hmph. I would've thought baseball with David on the team. But the season hadn't started yet. "Good idea. Sounds like it would be fun."

"Hey, what did you think of that algebra test? Kinda tough, huh?"

"Well, Jennifer used to tutor me in math just about every day, and we don't get together anymore, so ..." I tilted my head from side to side.

"Oh, that's too bad." The focus of her eyes shifted to the tree and back to me. "Um, I could try to help if you like."

"Really?" Why would she want to do that? "That's awfully nice of you."

"No problem. If you decide you want to get together for a session, call me and we'll see when we can meet." She wrote her number on a little notepad, tore off the sheet, and handed it to me.

"Thanks."

"Well, excuse me. I gotta go." She stood up and walked in the direction of the jocks near the steps.

Tookie joined the crowd of boys and placed a hand on the back of one who towered over her. The wall of bodies cracked opened and then closed again around her.

She was one of them. How'd she do that? She'd gained acceptance from them so easily and so quickly since school started. Most of those guys didn't know she existed a month ago.

I sighed. Some of us had to work harder at friendships than others did. And then we messed up some of the ones we'd gained.

The bell rang, and I rose to my feet to prepare for David. No matter what happened, I'd act like his friend.

Lucky break. I caught him at his locker on the way to my first class.

"Hi, David." I slowed down but didn't stop. Less confrontational. "I can't wait until February. How 'bout you?"

"February?"

"Well, yeah. Practice for baseball and track starts." I turned and walked backward, talking at the same time. "Did you forget?" I shouted the question.

David froze like a deer caught in headlights, unable to determine exactly what kind of creature he'd encountered. But at least he'd paid attention.

Things continued to go well. I didn't stalk him, but I didn't avoid him either. If I happened to see him, I nodded. Or smiled. Or said hi. When Tookie was with him, I acknowledged her too. I performed the courteous acts expected in civil society—picking up a dropped pen, reminding him of a book left on his desk. I became the cover girl for the good manners guide.

Acting like a polite acquaintance felt a whole lot better than acting like an enemy. I set my shoulders back and enjoyed breathing again.

By the dismissal bell, my step was lighter. When I joined Alice and Gayle at our lockers, hope for renewed friendship with David had replaced my despair. Totally.

"You look happy." Gayle smiled and leaned a shoulder against her closed locker, facing me. "I saw you talking to David during the day. What's going on?" She blinked.

"I'm making an effort to be nice." I grinned and sorted my books, selecting the ones to take home. "Hoping it'll pay off."

"If that's what you really want. But promise me you'll stay true to yourself." With a small intake of breath, her eyes opened wide and her mouth formed a small circle. "Oh, I didn't mean you aren't naturally nice!"

I burst out laughing. "Yeah, right."

She trotted down the hall, chuckling along the way.

Alice tilted her head and smiled. "You do deserve a guy who likes you just the way you are."

My heart filled with her sweetness. "Thanks, Alice." I smiled back.

Alice had proven to be more complicated than I'd given her credit for at first. Maybe she wanted the same thing for me that Gayle did, but I'd interpreted it all wrong.

She waited for me to secure my locker, and then we walked together to the bus.

While Alice and I boarded, David and his brother Ben crossed the parking lot beyond the loading zone. They headed toward Ben's car.

I chose a seat and looked out the window. The way David walked was so cute, the baseball player in him manifesting itself in the set of his shoulders and—aargh! Stop it.

I rotated my head until my neck popped and then faced the window again, hoping he'd gone.

Tookie darted across the parking lot after him like a cheetah after a gazelle. She caught his arm and showed him a piece of paper. Their heads tilted toward each other. He looked it over and nodded. She grinned and darted back in the direction she'd come.

I clenched my teeth. If he would only tell her to back off. *Stop it, Wendy.*

So my plan to re-friend David had hit a snag. The new and improved, amiable Tookie presented a challenge this go-round that didn't exist before. And she'd proven she was real. I'd experienced her myself. From all indication, he was interested. But so what?

If I wanted to be David's friend again, I'd have to learn to ignore Tookie's antics and not get jealous. I'd have to become even more amiable and easy going than Tookie.

But didn't David have a few things to learn too?

Chapter 23

My confidence sagging from Tookie saturation, I sat in the kitchen doing homework and eating an after-school snack with Adam.

The doorbell rang, and Mom answered it. "Well, hello. What a nice surprise." Muffled words. Then, "Wendy, someone's here to see you."

I lifted my head. Adam grinned, a new gap where he'd lost another tooth the night before.

A quick hop off the bar stool, a few long strides, and I was at the front door.

"Mrs. V!" I bounced twice on my toes. "It's great to see you!"

She smiled, eyes clear and bright. "Hello, Wendy." She wore a dress with coordinated costume jewelry and had done her makeup and styled her hair. She looked like herself.

My chest warmed. "Come in. Come in."

She stepped through the doorway.

I searched the driveway for her car. "How did you get here? Did you drive?" Worry creased my forehead.

"No—" she started, and then Tony stepped from behind the outside wall.

"Oh." My spirits sank. "Hello."

He nodded his head once. "She wanted to visit you. It was a good time for her, so ..."

"Thanks." I gave him a thin smile.

I took Mrs. V's hand and led her farther away from him.

"My rental car is parked on the street. I'll ride around and come back in about half an hour." Tony took a backward step.

"Nonsense," Mom said. "Come have some coffee."

"Thank you." He followed her.

I placed an arm around Mrs. V's shoulders. "Would you like to see my new room?"

She smiled. "I sure would."

Once inside, I moved clothes and books off my desk chair and offered her the seat. "Sorry about the mess. I usually don't tidy up until the weekend."

"No need to apologize. Your room is lovely, just like you are."

Sweet as always. "Thanks, but I wish my room could always be right next door to wherever you live."

"I appreciate your saying that, Wendy." She squeezed my hand.

"And it's not just because I love your cookies." I chuckled.

She crinkled her eyes. "You're like my own granddaughter, you know."

I grinned. "I'm glad, and I feel the same way." I dragged

the bench from the end of the bed toward her chair.

"I have a surprise." She reached inside her purse and extracted a tiny black velvet box. "For you."

"What's this?"

"Something to remember your surrogate grandmother by. And to reminisce about some of our good times together."

The box held a silver charm in the image of a puppy. It could've been Belle or Chanceaux.

I clutched the box to my chest. "I love it." Then I got down on my knees and hugged her.

She kissed the top of my head.

I placed the box on the desk, sat down again, and clasped my hands. "So you're leaving for Alaska soon, huh?" I did my best to use a light tone, not wishing to make either of us sad. We should enjoy each other while we could.

"Yes, this Sunday." Her voice was even. "I wanted to visit and talk to you while I can still think clearly. The doctors say that my cognitive ability will come and go for a while until the Alzheimer's gets bad." She held her head high and her expression steady.

She was amazing. If only I could be that brave and strong when I got sick or old. "I wish you didn't have to go so soon, but it means a lot to me that you came to see me today. I've missed you, and it's nice to see you alone." I slapped a hand over my mouth. "I didn't mean that the way it sounded."

"It's okay." She patted my knee. "Sam explained some

things to me that have happened. And he also told me you traveled to Bayou Calmon."

"Yes!" I brightened. "I found out about Andre and the scandal." I hopped off the bench and pulled the pink envelopes out of my desk drawer. Since Gayle's visit, I'd saved them in a neat stack tied together with string. "Look at these."

She stared at them for a second before taking the stack from my hand. Then she ran her fingers slowly over Andre's name without untying the string.

What was going through her mind? Was she still with me, or had she slipped into the past again?

She continued to stare at the stack of envelopes.

I spoke slowly at first, unsure if she comprehended me. "Andre's girlfriend, Clarisse, who became his wife, wrote these letters to him while they were apart. She became pregnant, but he never got to return home." I paused. "He died in a coal mine accident, Mrs. V."

Her head jerked up. She covered her mouth, a gurgling sound in her throat.

Her reaction was stronger than expected. She and Andre knew each other as kids, but …

She swallowed, her hand slipping down to her throat and remaining there. "I was afraid something tragic had happened to him. Of course, I'd heard the rumors he was seeing someone in secret that his parents didn't approve of. Then my family and I moved out of Louisiana for a while. I lost touch with your

Grand-mere soon after Andre left Bayou Calmon."

I took her other hand. "Were you close to him while you were growing up?"

She nodded and smiled a sad little smile. "You could say that, all right." She looked straight into my eyes. "I was the girl Andre was supposed to eventually marry. The one his family— your family—wanted him to marry."

I felt the blood drain from my face. Had my great-uncle hurt Mrs. V? "But I thought her name was Anita. I saw that in one of the letters."

"That was me—little Ana. Anita. That's what everyone called me. Everyone but your grandmother."

"O-o-oh." I hung my head and sighed. "I'm so sorry, Mrs. V." I searched her face. "Did you love him a lot?"

Her voice softened to almost a whisper. "I did, or I thought I did, very much. But I was young, much too young to know what real love was yet."

My heart ached for her. "That makes me want to cry." I threw my arms around her neck. She had suffered, and I knew what that suffering felt like.

She gently pulled my arms loose and shook her head. "No need to cry for me. Everything turned out just fine. It wasn't long before I met Gus, and I wouldn't trade the life I had with him for anyone else."

She hadn't known that Gus had been waiting for her, just around the corner of her life. Maybe there was someone waiting for me.

I smiled, for Mrs. V and for Gus. It must have been the right life for her. It resulted in Sam.

Chapter 24

Gayle slammed her locker door and faced me with her morning's load of books in her arms. "Let's go over to the football field after school and watch the boys practice. I can ask my mom to come pick us up and take us home afterward." Her eyes had that determination in them, the one that made me know she'd be a track star one day.

There was no use arguing. Besides, what better did I have to do? "Okay."

"Sounds good to me." Alice clicked her combination lock shut. "Wendy, would you see if your mom can meet Adam when he gets off the bus?"

"Sure." I sent a quick text.

We split up and headed to our homerooms.

During the day, David warmed up to Friendly Wendy a little at a time.

First thing was the smile from a distance—in front of school in the morning, in the halls between classes, across the cafeteria. Then a stop-and-chat at my desk in algebra and world history. Tookie took those classes at different times.

A bubble of hope for the future enveloped me as I climbed

into the stadium bleachers with Alice and Gayle after school. We sat low on the fifty yard line.

I stretched out my legs and propped my feet on the empty bleacher bench in front of me and opened a novel. May as well get some reading done.

Next to me, Gayle whispered to Alice as they both gazed out on the field.

I narrowed my eyes to pick out the object of their attention. A huge sophomore linebacker with a shaved brown head. A big bear kind of guy.

So that's why Gayle wanted to come today. She had a crush.

I slammed the book shut so I could observe. A potential first romance in our midst was better than one in a novel.

Grinning, I back-slapped Gayle's arm.

She turned with a guilty smile and shrugged. "I'll tell you about him later."

"I look forward to it." I wiggled my eyebrows.

We refocused on the field.

Wouldn't it be cool if Gayle and I both dated athletes? Sure, track was great, but to be in that enviable circle with football and baseball players ...

Our seat vibrated. Someone was joining us on our bench. I leaned backward to see past Alice and Gayle.

I bolted upright again.

David and Tookie. Did they go *everywhere* together, even

after school?

Alice and Gayle spoke to them. They returned a greeting.

David looked surprised to see me. Because it was a football practice?

Who knows.

Then he and Tookie put their heads together and began their own little whisper session.

My forehead tightened. He could've chosen to sit next to me. Or talk to me.

After trying as hard as I had to make him like me again, it was for nothing. He was still with Tookie.

So that was it. I slapped the bench next to my thigh. Short of strangling Tookie, there wasn't anything else I could do. I swallowed the sour lump in my throat. I didn't have the strength in me to fight for any guy.

Tookie had won by default.

That night, my phone rang, its new ringtone a clip of a tune by the Cajun band Beausoleil.

Dad.

"Hey, Wendy. How about I come pick you up tomorrow afternoon? Aunt Renee and the kids are driving over from Bayou Calmon."

Yay—Mattie! "That's sounds great, Dad."

Alice stood in my doorway, her eyes pleading. She pointed to her phone. "Jerome," she whispered.

I couldn't deprive her of an opportunity to see him.

"Dad, how about Alice too?"

"Of course she's welcome."

I smiled and nodded at Alice.

She shrieked and ran to her room.

Chapter 25

With the packet of pink envelopes tucked safely in Mattie's tote bag, she and I lounged on Dad's family room sofa with our feet propped on an ottoman. She rested her head comfortably against my arm.

As we agreed, Mattie would quietly return Clarisse's letters to the tool shed and place them back in the box with Andre's other belongings. Aunt Renee wouldn't know that they had ever been missing, if she was aware of their existence at all.

I could only assume that Aunt Renee had discovered and read one or more of the letters when she first received Andre's personal effects and before she stored the box in the shed. Knowing his death was sudden, she could have guessed why the last letter remained unopened if she'd seen it, but chose not to open it. If I'd been Aunt Renee, I might've been too sad to read any of the letters.

Grand-mere, Aunt Renee, and Dad watched me from a photo on Dad's fireplace mantel. If only I could tell what they knew.

Did Grand-mere, Aunt Renee, and Dad openly discuss Andre and Clarisse at any point, or did only whispers and rumors make their way to Dad? Maybe Aunt Renee and Dad would be willing to talk to each other about Andre and Clarisse, if they both knew the whole truth. Or talk to Jerome, Mattie, and me about the existence of our distant cousins. If not, the right time might come for me to ask Dad about Andre and bring the truth out in the open. But timing was everything, I'd learned.

Mattie turned her face up to mine, eyes big and pleading. "Would you play with my hair like last time?" She wore the blue ribbon I'd mailed back to her.

I chuckled. "Sure." I understood how addictive that indulgence could be.

She sighed and relaxed into the sofa cushions as I began working sections of hair and gliding them between my fingers.

Though clouds gathered in the sky, Jerome and Alice strolled past the front window toward the driveway, heading to the street.

Alone time. Nice.

They exchanged words known only to them, their faces inches apart. She smiled at him, her cheeks flushed.

Seeing her happy lifted my spirits. Jerome was so good for her, and I loved them both. I prayed their relationship would last until they could cross the miles on their own whenever they wanted to see each other.

But what about in between?

My fingers stopped their motion, and Mattie's hair slipped

from them.

I still had to live with Alice every day, whether she was happy or not.

Would she turn cold toward me again if I got another boyfriend and she couldn't be with Jerome? Or worse, if they broke up?

Something flip-flopped in my chest.

Would she look at me, his cousin, and see a glimpse of the boy who broke her heart?

I hadn't bargained for any of that before Mom remarried. Having a stepsister wasn't anything like I'd expected, any more than it was what Alice had hoped for. It involved risk. And mistakes. But that didn't necessarily mean it was bad.

I glanced at Mattie, her eyes closed. She'd enjoy having a sister, the step variety or not. And she needed one. She needed *me*. I should ask Dad to arrange for Mattie to spend some time with me on a regular basis.

I sighed and relaxed my shoulders.

Maybe the relationship between every two sisters was different, whether they were stepsisters or related by blood. No two girls were alike, no matter what. If I had a real sister, we'd probably have the same kinds of disagreements Alice and I had—about boys and broken commitments—and in the future, about sharing a car and lots more.

All I could do was wait and see if Alice and I would work things out.

Chapter 26

I nestled Mrs. V's favorite hat on her head, a sassy blue one with a peacock feather on the side.

With Tony's permission, I'd styled her hair, applied her makeup, and helped her dress for the trip to Alaska. I'd set aside her wool coat so it wouldn't be packed. The daytime temperature in Anchorage was already near freezing, and she'd need a coat as soon as she arrived.

She and I turned together toward her dresser mirror. "You look beautiful, Mrs. V."

She smiled at me, but only the same polite smile she gave the healthcare worker who'd visited earlier. That was okay, because she made me smile. Always.

"Is it all right if I hug you?" I hesitated. Sudden actions frightened her.

She didn't refuse, so I enclosed her in my arms and gently rubbed her back. "I love you, Mrs. V." I spoke softly against her cheek. "Sam will let me know how you're doing, and maybe you can talk to me on the phone sometime." I held a sliver of hope that her recent period of clarity would repeat—and often.

Sam looked on, tight-lipped, his eyes now a cloudy

golden-brown and misted over. He couldn't have read most of what I said, only my body language.

I let go and handed Mrs. V her purse, willing myself not to cry. She needed me to be the strong one.

Sam lifted Mrs. V's coat off the bed. "Dad said I can ride with you, if that's okay."

I nodded. "Of course. I don't think Mom will mind either."

He took a deep breath. "It's time."

We led Mrs. V into the living room where Tony waited for her.

Sam and I rode in the backseat of Mom's car, with Mom as chauffeur. Neither Papa D nor Alice insisted on accompanying us. They seemed to know this trip was highly personal.

After a few minutes on the road, with me staring out my window, Sam spoke. "How are you feeling?"

I swallowed hard and turned to him. "Honestly? I feel like I'll never see either one of you again, and it makes me sad. Sadder than I've ever been." I didn't have anything further to lose, so I might as well tell the truth.

He squinted that eye. "Friends don't have to live next door to each other, you know. Or even within forty five hundred miles."

I grinned in spite of myself.

"You and Grandma will always be friends. *We'll* always be friends. Besides, I wouldn't count on you and me never seeing each other again." He smiled.

I inhaled a small, joyful breath. His optimism was catching, and a reminder. You never know what the future will hold. If anyone should understand that, I should.

Theory and reality don't coexist when you're saying good-bye to two people you care about.

It took every ounce of self-control to remain calm at the airport when Tony led Mrs. V away to wait in the check-in line. It was a good thing for me she didn't look back. She didn't remember who I was.

Mom stood a distance from Sam and me and pretended to study the terminal architecture while dabbing her nose with a tissue.

Sam took both my hands in his. "It's been great knowing you." When he said it, it didn't sound like some line a guy would say. "I'll miss you, Wendy."

He leaned over and I raised my face. He touched the briefest kiss to my lips.

I smiled. "Take care, Sam. I'll see you someday in Alaska." I believed it.

He squinted that hawk eye and walked away, rolling his luggage behind him.

Chapter 27

I traveled in silence on the return home from the airport, my breathing so shallow it didn't make a sound.

When traffic lightened enough for Mom to take her eyes off the road, she glanced over to check on me. I granted her a weak smile. Her eyes were still puffy like mine.

Finally, we turned into our old neighborhood and in a few minutes onto Mrs. V's driveway. I reached behind me for the dog leash on the backseat, and my hand touched something paper.

It was a large manila envelope with a metal clasp. On the outside, someone had printed "Wendy." I undid the clasp and pulled out the contents. It was the drawing of Mrs. V and me. No note was attached. None was needed. Mrs. V's face and Sam's signature communicated everything.

Chanceaux's bark drew me to her. She ran along the fence on the side next to my old yard, excited by the two little kids playing there.

I sighed, glad my old house wasn't lonely anymore. The azaleas bloomed to prove that happiness dwelt there.

"Come on, Chanceaux." I unlatched and pushed her

squeaky chain-link gate open.

She rushed toward me, stopping inches from my shoes. She wagged her tail and nuzzled my leg.

"Time to go to your new home." I fought back tears as I clipped the leash to her collar.

A glimmer of confusion passed through her big brown eyes. Maybe someone like David who didn't understand dogs wouldn't have noticed, but I did.

"Nobody lives here now, girl." I cleared my throat. "But your daughter Belle is waiting for you."

I loaded her into the backseat of the car and stroked under her muzzle to reassure her that everything would be all right. Just different.

Different. Like it always was for me. Ever changing. Gain someone new one day, lose someone else the next. Repeat.

"Home, safe and sound," Mom said as she eased the car into our garage.

And it finally *was* starting to feel like home. For Mom and me, for all five of us together, safe and sound. With love for one another, tested but not destroyed.

I led Chanceaux through the garage and into the kitchen. "It may take a little while to get used to the place, but you'll like it here."

Belle appeared out of nowhere and bounded up to Chanceaux. Both tails quivered in recognition.

I removed the leash, and the two dogs took off to the

living room. I followed the voices floating toward me.

My eyes slowly adjusted to the darkened room, the only light coming from the TV. Two heads sharpened into focus above the back of the sofa. Alice and—

"David?"

He turned and rose from his seat, Alice from hers.

I looked from one to the other. What were they doing here together? They'd barely tolerated each other when I wanted them to.

As though reading my mind, David said, "Alice thought you might need some cheering up."

All my disappointments gathered into a huge swell of tears that threatened to crack the wall I'd built around my heart. I chewed my lip. I wouldn't allow myself to break down in front of him.

His voice softened. "Look, I know I was wrong to act the way I did. I shouldn't try to tell you who you can be friends with. All I care about is that you and I are still friends." His face was as open and honest as a puppy's.

But was he saying that only because Sam was no longer a threat?

He stepped closer to stand a foot in front of me. "And I'm sorry."

I took a shaky breath. "I shouldn't have expected you never to speak to Tookie again either."

He offered his palm to me.

How could I be mean to him? I covered his palm with mine.

Alice gave me a thumbs-up and scurried from the room.

"Tookie's only a friend, like I said. She decided she's more interested in one of the football players—"

"And she convinced you to help her get together with him."

He grinned and shrugged.

"You little cupid, you." I gently poked his stomach.

Belle sauntered up to David, her tail swishing.

He took a half-step back. "Does Belle have a leash?"

"Why?" Did he think I'd restrain her in my own house?

He tilted his head and smiled. "I thought we'd take both dogs for a walk."

I threw my arms around his shoulders and plastered my cheek against his chest. "That sounds wonderful."

Final step toward achieving girlfriend status:

10. Becoming real friends (Check.)

List of Resources

The following resources are for the reader's convenience and do not signify endorsement. Many resources are available online and from public and school libraries, guidance counselors, and doctors' offices and clinics.

When someone close to you has Alzheimer's

AFA Teens: http://www.afateens.org/coping.html

Alzheimer's Association: Kids & Teens:
http://www.alz.org/living_with_alzheimers_just_for_ki
ds_and_teens.asp

Coping with Blended Families/Stepfamilies

KidsHealth: TeensHealth: Stepparents:
http://kidshealth.org/teen/your_mind/Parents/stepparen
ts.html

Dating for the First Time

Momsmack: 11 Things Girls Should Know Before
Their First Date: http://momsmack.com/11-things-
girls-should-know-before-their-first-date/

Discussion Questions

1. Make a list of steps you would have to achieve before you would consider yourself someone's girlfriend. How does your list compare with Wendy's?

2. Name one character that had different expectations from a relationship with Wendy than Wendy did. What was the difference in expectations, and did they resolve their differences? If so, how? If not, why not?

3. Name a character that was not a blood relative of Wendy's but that she considered family. How did she show her feelings? Should she have done more to express her fondness?

4. Do you think it is possible that Wendy held equally strong feelings for David and for Sam? Should she have chosen to spend time with only one of them? Why or why not?

5. Concerning secret history of ancestors, is it possible to be too nosy? How do you relate to Wendy's desire to find out what happened to her great-uncle?

6. What made Wendy's friendships with Alice and Gayle work?

About the Author

Cynthia is a former advertising designer, marketing director, and interior decorator who holds a BA in art education with a minor in history. While employed by a large daily newspaper, she tried to rewrite some ad copy without permission and got into trouble for it. At that point, she knew she was destined to become an author.

When she's not cooking Cajun or Italian food, Cynthia writes historical and contemporary teen fiction containing elements of mystery and romance. Her debut novel, *Bird Face*, won a 2014 Moonbeam Children's Book Award, Bronze, in the Pre-teen Mature Issues category. That book became *8 Notes to a Nobody*, book one of The Bird Face Series published by Write Integrity Press.

Cynthia has a passion for rescuing dogs from animal shelters and studying the history of the friendly southern U.S. from Georgia to Texas, where she resides with her husband and several canines.

Connect with Cynthia online:

Website:	www.CynthiaTToney.com
Blog:	www.BirdFaceWendy.wordpress.com
Facebook:	www.facebook.com/BirdFaceWendy
Twitter:	**@CynthiaTToney**

Book One of the Bird Face Series

Available Now!

Thanks for reading our books!

Look for other books

published by

www.WriteIntegrity.com

and

Pix-N-Pens Publishing

www.PixNPens.com

Made in the USA
Coppell, TX
13 December 2024